The Third Day of September Ides

Book One:

So, you say, we need a disaster

The Third Day of September Ides

Book One:

So, you say, we need a disaster

✦ ✦ ✦

by Ely Asher

Galiel.Net
Seattle

The Third Day of September Ides, Book One: So, you say, we need a disaster *by Ely Asher*

All Right Reserved © 2004 by Ely Asher

No part of this book may be reproduced or transmitted in any form or by any means, graphic, electronic, or mechanical, including photocopying, recording, taping, or by any information storage or retrieval system, without the permission in writing from the copyright owner.

This publication is designed to provide accurate and authoritative information with regard to the subject matter covered. It is sold with the understanding that the publisher and the author(s) are not engaged in rendering legal, accounting, or other professional advice. If legal advice or other expert assistance is required, the services of a competent professional person should be sought.

Galiel.Net and the author(s) have endeavored to provide trademark information about all the companies and products mentioned in this book by the appropriate use of capitals. However, we cannot guarantee the accuracy of this information. All the names used in this book are either historical or fictional. Any similarities to the names of real people who lived after A.D. II, if any, are purely accidental.

For sales, information and questions on rights and permissions contact:
Galiel.Net
704 228th Ave. NE, # 173
Sammamish, WA 98074-7222
http://www.Galiel.Net
Sales@Galiel.Net

ISBN-13: 978-0-9770364-2-4
ISBN: 0-9770364-2-1
Library of Congress Control Number: 2005939156
Printed in the United States of America

> "The first duty of a citizen is to question motives of his government."
> —Folklore, attributed to Thomas Jefferson

> "To announce that there must be no criticism of the President or that we are to stand by the President right or wrong is not only unpatriotic and servile but it is morally treasonable to the American public."
> —Theodore Roosevelt, 1918, Republican President

Verbum Sapienti Sat Est

Ancient Rome, early spring A.D. 64, alternate universe…

Some history-literate readers will say that the story does not reflect true historic events. "Hey, Rome did not depend on olive oil from Greece! And anyway, how can oil prices get an empire into economical trouble? D'oh!... Not **that** oil!"

The answer is simple: this is an alternate universe, where anything is possible. And if you don't see a connection with our world, maybe it's because there is none. Or maybe it's because you just don't see it.

But let's get to the story, in which the prefect of Praetorian Guards has a problem and the Emperor finds a solution.

Table of Content

SO, YOU SAY, WE NEED A DISASTER Chapter I, where the prefect of Praetorian Guards has a problem and the emperor finds a solution 7

NOTHING BUT TROUBLE Chapter II, where we meet Nil and he gets a mission he does not completely comprehend 12

LORD, SAVE YOUR GOOD SHEEP Chapter III, where we observe a theological dispute on whether killing people is good 18

CAN WE BURN HIS HOUSE, PLEASE? Chapter IV, where doctor Noot gets a bit more than he had asked for 24

WE ARE HELPING THE EMPEROR, PACHO! Chapter V, where Nil looks for a pleasure and finds a ship and information. 30

JUST IN CASE Chapter VI, where Nil gets a new name and a death sentence in absentia 38

SURE THING, GLAP Chapter VII, where we learn that there is a lot to loot in Rome and that Drakon knows how to be grateful 43

IF WE ARE FAITHFUL ENOUGH Chapter VIII, where Nil meets a clever zealot and the zealot meets a stupid Roman 51

THOSE SLY BASTARDS Chapter IX, where we learn how disaster may be a source of hefty profits 57

LOVE THY NEIGHBOR Chapter X, where we learn some exotic reasons for love 64

I'LL SEND THE PEOPLE Chapter XI, where, for a change, we meet two people who don't want Rome to burn 74

A PROVINCE, YOU WON'T MISS Chapter XII, where we see what is the use of being the emperor's wife 81

THAT REQUIRES SOME MONEY Chapter XIII, where Nil gets help that many would not expect 87

BROTHERS IN CHRIST, SMILE! Chapter XIV, where we learn how to expose Christians in their own words ... 95

LOCAL STINKERS DON'T COUNT Chapter XV, where one Roman, one Greek, and one Egyptian are looking for one Christian Jew and cannot find him 102

TRUST THE LORD Chapter XVI, where Gessimus Florus gets a province, and Bin Jamen a.k.a. Nil gets a ghostwriter 112

I GUESS NOT, YOUR HONOR Chapter XVII, where Nil meets a not-very-good-Christian in the land that does not care about Rome 120

IT BECOMES A HABIT Chapter XVIII, where Nil sees a black cat in a dark room 131

OH, SHIT! Chapter XIX, where Nil hears a lot of things he finds hard to believe 135

EMPEROR THE WHO? Chapter XX, where senator Albinus is not happy with the emperor and Nil learns to master the roads 154

ZE GRIEF OF YOUR PEOPLE Chapter XXI, where the wish of so many comes true 164

SO, YOU SAY, WE NEED A DISASTER
Chapter I, where the prefect of Praetorian Guards has a problem and the emperor finds a solution

Ancient Rome, early spring A.D. 64, alternate universe...

Some history-literate readers will say that the story does not reflect true historic events. "Hey, Rome did not depend on olive oil from Greece! And anyway, how can oil prices get an empire into economical trouble? D'oh!... Not *that* oil!"

The answer is simple: this is an alternate universe, where anything is possible. And if you don't see a connection with our world, maybe it's because there is none. Or maybe it's because you just don't see it.

But let's get to the story, in which the prefect of Praetorian Guards has a problem and the Emperor finds a solution.

* * *

Roman nights are chilly in the early spring, but it did not bother the guests in the sumptuous imperial palace on Palatine Hill. Hot air from the basement warmed every room including a large *triclinium* filled with noble guests and some lesser folk. To tell the truth, not all the guests were so noble. *O tempora, O mores!* The dinner had just started so their garments still were clean, but there was no clean soul, no noble man, no unsoiled woman in the room. How had they become the emperor's guests? Who cares? Certainly, that's not the emperor who just left his guests for the privacy of his *tablinum*, the study room.

Right after him, another guest left the room. Albeit "guest" was not the right word for Ophonius Tigellinus. The prefect of Praetorian Guards was almost as much the master in the palace as the emperor himself.

These two had a good reason to neglect food, wine, and guests. Praetorian Guards represented both the intelligence and the secret police of the vast empire, and the emperor wanted a report.

"Should I start with the best or with the worst?" Tigellinus asked.

"Worst," the emperor said firmly and waved his hand toward the door. "I can get good news from those jesters in the triclinium."

Tigellinus chuckled with content and said, "The worst news is that Greek olive oil prices went up."

"Why should I care about olive oil prices?" the emperor asked. "What am I, a poor shoemaker?"

"You should not," Tigellinus agreed. "But you should care about shoemakers and the rest of the plebs. They care about olive oil, because that's what they eat every day with their bread."

The emperor shrugged his shoulders and said, "Fine, and why did the price go up?"

"First, the Greeks had bad weather last year," Tigellinus said. "Second, they hate us. So for them overpricing us is like killing two Persians with one arrow."

"Can't we just send a few legions there?" the emperor asked.

"We already have several legions in Greece, Caesar," Tigellinus said, "but it does not make them love us. Besides, you cannot wage a war over a few lousy *sesterces*. Great minds like you understand the importance of olive oil prices, but would patricians understand it? You'll be laughed at by the people of Rome. They will say that you bring an olive branch of war."

"You're right," the emperor agreed. "It's so disgusting to rule over people who only think of oil and bread. Speaking of bread, at least it's coming to Rome uninterrupted, right?"

"Yes, Caesar," Tigellinus said. "Egypt sees us dead every night in their dreams, but they are too afraid to disobey."

"Yes, I've got it," the emperor said. "So who else likes us a lot?"

"Everyone," Tigellinus said. "Gauls, Germans, Numidians, Jews… Speaking of Jews, we are not on top of their tetrarchs' agenda."

"How sweet!" the emperor said sarcastically. "So who has topped us on their hate list?"

"Christians," Tigellinus said. "That's their new sect. Jewish tetrarchs feel threatened by them. Granted, Christians don't like

Rome either. They say you are the essence of evil and that soon you will be beaten by their good guy."

"And who would that be?" the emperor asked, sniffing scornfully.

"Some guy we crucified by decision of their own court about 30 years ago," Tigellinus said indifferently. "They also say that Rome is the Capital of Evil and that Rome will be destroyed. They also deny your divine nature."

"That's what all Jews do, right?"

"Kind of," Tigellinus agreed. "Strange, I never thought about that before. I guess regular Jews don't deny you so annoyingly as those Christians. Except for their other sect, those zealots. They are calling for a revolt. Poor things..."

"Whatever," said the Emperor with a dismissive wave. "So what else is going well?"

"We've caught and executed the head of the Sicilian pirates," Tigellinus answered.

"Those contrabandists who avoid paying customs and fill Rome with cheap Greek wine and Eastern opium?"

"The same and the only, Caesar," Tigellinus confirmed. "Of course, now all their families have sworn to kill you, me, and destroy Rome... some day, but what can they do? They are lucky enough to get past my guards into the city, only it would not be wise for them to push their luck too far."

"So what happened between you and him?" the emperor asked, narrowing his eyes at the prefect. "Just the truth, Ophonius, all I need is the plain truth. I can invent lies myself. I know he paid you for years so that you would let him go on with his little business."

Tigellinus' eyes betrayed his confusion, but he pulled himself together and said quietly, "He skipped several payments. I warned him, but he did not listen."

The emperor shrugged his shoulders indifferently and said, "So, what else?"

"Same old, same old," Tigellinus said. "Barbarians attack our northern borders, Mauritanian Berbers occasionally rob trade ships, Parthians don't want to give Armenia back, but overall nothing much to worry about. Nobody outside can really challenge us, Caesar, though many try."

"So many provinces, so many satellites, and all of them wish us dead." The emperor sighed.

"What do you want? We are the greatest empire on Earth, Caesar. Empires have provinces, empires have satellites, and empires have other enemies. Empires never have friends – none but ourselves."

"I wonder why they have not burned Rome yet," the emperor said.

"Keeping in mind what we are going to discuss next," Tigellinus answered with a chuckle, "I wonder why you have not burned Rome yet."

The emperor looked at him with a calm surprise.

"Domestic affairs," the prefect said.

"What about them?" the emperor asked.

"Starting from small stuff," Tigellinus said, "this Jewish sect gets a lot of followers in Rome. You know, the ones who deny you and want to see Rome destroyed. The Christians."

"So? Don't tell me you cannot handle them."

"There are too many," Tigellinus said. "Massacre will not make you more popular, Caesar. Granted, they are just a little annoyance, but they poison the public with all the hate tales about you."

"Public?" the emperor asked, raising a brow.

"The public is nothing, but it can be used against you, Caesar," Tigellinus answered, "And the public is not very fond of you. People talk about Agrippina and Octavia—"

"She was conspiring against me, you know that!" the emperor said.

"I know," Tigellinus said apologetically. "But still, Agrippina was your mother, and the public did not like what you did."

"Why can't they just shut up and get over it?" the emperor asked.

"They would, but you know, that price of olive oil makes them look for a reason to dislike you," Tigellinus answered. "And somebody can try to use that."

"Who? The public does not matter, and I can execute any patrician just on suspicion," the Emperor said.

"Say, Gaius Calpurnius does not look very happy. And what about your teacher, Seneca? Did he really retire, or did he just take some time to make new plans? And what about Petronius, that *Arbiter Elegantiae* of yours?"

"What about them?" the emperor asked scornfully. "Three emperors in a row – Claudius, Caligula, and Tiberius – were killed by Praetorian Guards, and you are backing me up. What can those patricians do?"

"What about Julius Caesar?" Tigellinus asked. "Don't give your enemies a weapon against you. Don't let them feed on public opinion. We can't even execute them on the spot, because then the public would turn on you even more, and you would only get more enemies."

"Fine, so what are you getting at?" the emperor asked.

"Two things," Tigellinus said. "We need to make you popular, and we need the people's attention off the current problems. And this must be big. Say, if you'd save the city from some imminent danger or catastrophe, then everything would be different. I'd be able to execute any of your enemies on the spot, and the crowd would cheer up. You'd be able to send legions wherever you want, and everybody would applaud you."

"But what can I save the city from?" the emperor asked. "All these enemies inside and abroad haven't done anything serious yet."

"You almost wish their wishes would come true," Tigellinus said. Then he chuckled and looked at the emperor. A soft silence filled the room broken only by voices coming from the triclinium. Both men were thinking.

"So, you say we need a disaster," said the emperor at last, quietly.

* * *

Modern history is certain that early Christians had nothing to do with burning Rome in A.D. 64. Many historians also agree that Emperor Nero had nothing to do with it as well.

NOTHING BUT TROUBLE
Chapter II, where we meet Nil and he gets a mission he does not completely comprehend

The Middle East was always nothing but trouble for the empire, thought the lone rider going down Appian Way. Two narrow stripes of purpure on his tunic, partially visible inside a military *lacerna* cloak, revealed him as a member of the Equestrian Order–a respectable class serving the empire right between the senators and everybody else. Originally a Roman cavalry of the Republic, the *equites* gave up most of their military functions to regiments of horsemen from the Eastern provinces and became heart and brain of the imperial machine. Equites commanded legions, managed public property, and occasionally even governed some provinces. That's not to mention such mundane affairs as administration, supplies, or security.

The latter was the area chosen by the rider. He looked on the right at the pastoral landscape of the hills of southern Italy. The sun was setting. A tall stone tomb stood near the road, one side decorated with a large rainwater bowl. Scarlet and gold reflections flickered in the water like flame. They reminded the rider of the subject of his recent conversation and, after a while, he concluded his thought – now Egyptian priests are going to burn Rome.

Nil Nihil Septimus, eques, son and grandson of equites, great grandson of a Julius Caesar legionnaire, was the seventh son in a large and not very wealthy family. When he was born, his father sighed and said, "With so many brothers and sisters, he is nothing and he will achieve nothing, and what is especially bad, he is the seventh of nothings." This is how he got his name.

Contrary to his father's fears, Nil took his words as a blessing and chose a career where being nothing and invisible was the most important skill to survive and succeed. He became a secret agent of the empire. Now he was going on the most unusual assignment of his life. Nil started to recollect the conversation with the prefect.

Nil had had a good career. He reported directly to the prefect of Praetorian Guards, who was the head of imperial police, security, intelligence, and counter-intelligence in one person. Some assignments required traveling, and some kept him in the city, in which case greater precautions to maintain secrecy were needed. His latest assignment was of the latter kind. His orders were to keep an eye on a new religious sect spreading across Rome like a wild fire, so to allow members of this sect to see him entering the emperor's palace was not a very good idea. Of course, it would not be a disaster either. After all, they had their people in the palace anyway, and they would be glad to have one more follower there. The problem with that was that Nil wanted to use these people for his and the empire's advantage, not the other way around. So he was not surprised when, one morning, a soldier came to his house with a message that he should go to a secluded villa about 15 miles to the south from the city walls along Appian Way.

A barefoot slave girl in a short off-white tunic showed Nil inside, and relieved him of his dusty cloak and military *caliga* sandals. Then she washed his feet with aromatic water and slipped soft indoor sandals on them. Such an outstanding reception was not totally unusual in Rome, but it was unusual for Nil's meeting with the prefect. The girl led him into the triclinium–the dining room–with an open window looking into the olive garden outside. The prefect of Praetorian Guards, Ophonius Tigellinus, lay stretched leisurely on the coach, enjoying the scenery. Nil stood straight, looking at his boss, and Tigellinus, with a waive of the hand, pointed to another couch across the table. It had to be something important. Nil thanked the prefect, laid down comfortably, and accepted a goblet of wine poured by the girl.

"There are several reasons why I wanted to talk to you, Nil," said Tigellinus. "First, tell me about the flock you are herding for us. I mean this Jewish sect, the Christians. Or should I say 'the pack'?"

"Why–" started Nil, but broke off his question "I apologize, prefect. Of course, it's a flock. They are sheep; stupid, submissive sheep. Sure, they believe that Rome is evil, but they are not going to do anything about it. They believe that any

13

authority is from their god, so they should tolerate it. Slaves are more rebellious than they are."

"Did you hear anything that might indicate criminal action or intent against the emperor or the empire?" Tigellinus took a pickled olive, closed his eyes, and sipped the wine.

"No, nothing real," said Nil after a pause. "Sure, there is Seamus and his men. They are like a sect within a sect. Most Christians fear them. Seamus says that instead of waiting for Rome to be destroyed, they should destroy it themselves. But there is little danger of that. There are too few of them, and most Christians don't agree. None of them have the guts to play with fire."

"Interesting that you mention fire," said Tigellinus, without opening his eyes. "How can you be so sure?"

"It was an expression... but, anyway, Seamus' people are idiots. And Seamus is the biggest idiot of all. He'll have an accident and set his own tunic on fire, before burning anything else."

"And still your sheep are going to burn Rome..." Tigellinus opened his eyes and looked sharply at Nil. "Yes, Nil, Rome."

"With all due respect, prefect, how can they set fire to the whole city? They are just not qualified. Thinking of that, nobody is. Burning the city is not like burning a single house. You need to set fire in many different places at the same time. Then you need to prevent people and firefighters from putting out the fire. And you need to do that with guards all around the city. Vigilantes and Praetorians will catch them immediately. Even with a smaller city, you have to conquer it first to burn it."

"Throughout history, whole cities have been burned to the ground," Tigellinus said.

"Yes, prefect, by acts of gods," Nil said. "But we are looking for somebody on earth, right?"

"Think again, Nil. Somebody is going to burn Rome." Tigellinus put extra stress on 'is', but Nil did not understand why. The prefect continued. "I think maybe your Christians. If you think differently, tell me who?"

Nil shook his head.

"Think of it as having already happened. Now you need to put the blame on someone and make the people of Rome believe you," Tigellinus suggested.

Nil thought for a moment. "It takes somebody as skillful as Egyptian priests to accomplish arson on such a scale. They are close to their gods and they hate us. Anybody else would not be believable."

"And who said Christians cannot employ the help of Egyptian priests?" the prefect said, smiling, relaxed again.

Nil was confused. For all he knew, the prefect's words did not make any sense. But he was a military man, so instead of trying to crack the riddle, he just asked, "I apologize for my stupidity, but can you explain how Christians might persuade Egyptians to do such a work for them?"

"Christians are the Jewish sect. I remember you told me that Jews spent a lot of time in Egypt in the past."

"Yes, they did, according to their books," Nil said.

"And I remember they weren't the lowest people there, right?"

"Yes, prefect. According to their books, the first Jew in Egypt became the second person in the land after the pharaoh himself. And the last of their leaders there was a foster son of the pharaoh. However, in the very end he had to take his people by force, almost a war, because the pharaoh, his foster brother, did not want to let them go."

"History has seen worse things when two brothers faced a single throne to inherit," Tigellinus said, smiling. "But do you think the link between Jewish and Egyptian priests was broken because two brothers were at war for the throne?"

Nil first went blank but then brightened with understanding. "No way, prefect. Of course they have connections to each other! I never thought about it before, but after you put it so simply..." Nil paused. "So, you said they are going to burn Rome? Dirty dogs!"

"Relax, Nil. The empire is strong. We can handle a few nuts here and there." Tigellinus waived his hand and slaves brought two new dishes with grilled meat, fresh bread, and more wine. "Let's enjoy the meal and talk about something different. By the way, I highly recommend the meat. My cook prepares pork as nobody else can."

"For your generous patronage! Live long, prefect!" Nil raised a goblet and drank it. After all, if his commanding officer wanted to be friendly, all the better. The meat was indeed good.

Tigellinus accepted the praise with a nod and continued. "His former owner would never let him go. Lucky for me, the son of the owner was indiscreet in public." Nil smiled to show his understanding of how costly indiscreet words about authorities could be. Tigellinus went on, "So I let the young man go, and he let the cook go. The cook was worth it. His only problem is that he likes to spend time in the city. And you know what people say about the emperor in the city. I don't want him to get ideas like that. After all, I am the prefect of Praetorian Guards; I cannot let my slaves offend Divine Augustus."

"They are pigs, prefect!" Nil said. "The emperor gives them food and arranges the games, but they still don't like him. Only pigs could be so ungrateful!"

"Take it easy, Nil. They are still Roman citizens," Tigellinus said. "I have to admit, except for his poetic exercises, the emperor lately has had too few opportunities to show his glory. How can they love him if they don't have proof of his greatness?"

"The emperor does not need any proof," Nil cautiously argued. The prefect's statement was too close to the elusive boundary of an offense to the emperor and, in fact, already beyond it. Nil knew that. After all, he was a Praetorian Guard and a secret agent.

"Of course, he does not," Tigellinus agreed with a dismissive wave of his hand. "But the crowd does. You know these low-lifes. It's almost a pity that your arsonists don't have the slightest chance of succeeding. Imagine how popular the emperor would become if he had to cope with the results of such a disaster, saving people from hunger, providing shelter, and most importantly," Tigellinus raised a finger, "finding and punishing the guilty."

"Yes," Nil agreed. "After that, they would be more respectful."

"It's strange that the enemies can do such a great service to the empire, while we have to prevent them from doing it." Tigellinus paused, thoughtfully looking at the garden behind the window.

"Friends can betray, but enemies are always loyal," Nil said, breaking the uneasy silence with an old joke.

"True, my friend," Tigellinus agreed and raised a goblet. "For the real loyalty."

Nil nodded and drank his wine. They kept silent for a while.

"To the business, Nil," Tigellinus said at last. "How do you want to take care of your Judo-Egyptian incendiaries?"

"I've already thought about it a bit," Nil said, as he understood that the prefect asked for a plan. "I think no Egyptian priests have visited Rome lately. Hence, Christians could not contact them in the city. That means it's likely they sent somebody to Egypt. You need to alert guards and vigilantes against Egyptian priests coming to the city. Meanwhile, I'll go to Egypt. It could not be their high priests. Their high priests fear us, so they cooperate. It's somebody lower and less visible. I'll go to our procurator of Egypt and we will talk to the high priests. They will help us find the culprits."

"Good, good," Tigellinus said with a nod. "Depart first thing tomorrow morning. I'll take care of things in the city. One more thing, what if Egyptians don't really plan to burn Rome?"

Nil froze, looking at his boss. What does he mean, "don't plan?" Didn't Tigellinus just say that they did? Then understanding struck Nil. Of course, they would deny any knowledge!

"Don't worry, prefect," Nil said firmly, "I'll make sure, they do."

LORD, SAVE YOUR GOOD SHEEP
Chapter III, where we observe a theological dispute on whether killing people is good

If you think Italy is warm, think again. Southern Italy, maybe, but Rome? The chill of an early spring night easily gets under a tunica, even if you can afford two or three of them. That night in Rome many people leaving the city and going up *Via Salaria* – the Salt Way – had only one tunic under their hooded cloaks, but something important made them bear the cold and continue on toward their mysterious goal. Some of them were hiding oil lanterns under the laps of their cloaks, but most relied on the full moon shining from the clear night sky. A couple of miles past the remnants of the city wall, they turned right into an old cemetery located among sandy hills and ravines.

The crowd assembled in an area paved with limestone and surrounded by walls. In the center of it, an old crypt stood lost and forgotten. Several people started a bonfire near it, and the flame threw warm yellow reflections on the stones, which were silvery in the moonlight. When the stream of people let up, the gathering started to sing a hymn.

A lonely traveler might be frightened by such a scene, but his fear would be needless. These were the followers of a strange eastern religion that considered murder to be the mortal sin. That night, in the first century A.D., they had not yet become the world's dominating religion. The hooves of the crusaders' horses had not yet been covered in the blood of people and the chips of crosses from Constantinople temples. Incas and Mayas in South America were gathering gold, unaware of whose hands it would end up in. North American tribes were hunting and gathering, unaware of the people with faces colored by death. Neither were the African people, who did not even think of leaving the pastures of their native continent. Rifles had not yet been invented, nor had guns, planes, nuclear bombs, aircraft carriers, or other various smart and precise weapons designed to interrupt somebody else's unholy or merely inconvenient life. These were early Christians, trusting the Lord, shying at sins, and trying to follow the Commandments to the best of their human ability. They were still united. A Roman Christian would not hesitate to help his Greek brother, if the need arose, and it was the same the other way around. Unfortunately, this was not to last.

After the singing was over, people began to talk to each other, gravitating toward two of their leaders. The first was a tall strong man, about thirty years old, with fair hair and fiery eyes. If not for a wide scar on the right half of his forehead, he might have posed for a sculpture of Apollo. Son of the chief of a small Germanic tribe, he had been captured in a distant *Gallia Comata*, brought to Rome as a slave, and then forced to fight in the arena. He was a good fighter and soon became the favorite of the crowd, especially the women. Eventually he was set free like the legendary Spartacus. Soon after that, he was injured in a street fight, which explained both his scar and his clumsiness when he moved about. The blow to his head also had an unexpected consequence. The man started to hear voices telling him what to do. Soon, he became a Christian and gained substantial influence over the community with his fierce faith and strange link to the world beyond. People came to him, listened, asked questions, and then left to give the place for others, except for a small group of about a dozen most loyal followers.

The second leader, a lean gray-haired man in his early fifties, was wrapped in a hooded gray cloak. He listened more than he spoke, while intently looking at the people with large, dark, and vivid eyes. When he did speak, everybody around listened to his quiet, confident voice in silence. He had been brought from Greece as a slave and a teacher of Greek, Latin, and rhetoric. When his master set him free, he chose to stay with his former master and continue to do what he did so well – teach rhetoric. He clearly did know it well. People came to him, asked questions, listened to his answers, and followed him.

As the two leaders walked among the people, they drew closer and closer together. Soon they met, and then everyone's attention focused on them. They did not say anything for a few seconds, then the older man broke the silence.

"So, Seamus, I see we must talk. You chose the time when neither Peter nor Paul were in the city, so talk to me. What do you want?"

Seamus, the tall, younger leader, said, "Only to fulfill our Lord's will, Alexius!"

"And what would that be?" the old man asked, without moving a muscle in his face.

"You know what it is. Rome is an unclean place. Rome sends legions to our lands and you know what they do there. Rome made us slaves, and even when it sets us free, we are not much better off. The Romans are disgusting and immoral. They see the whole world as their slaves! Rome stands against everything we believe in. Rome must be destroyed, burned to the ground. You were a slave once, Alexius. Did you like it?"

Seamus' followers started to shout their support, but Alexius did not move. Then, when the noise of the crowd died down, he said, "No, I did not. But I knew that it was not just fate. Our Lord wanted me to learn something important. Maybe by complying with my master, I could learn to comply with our Lord? Could it be that He wants you to learn something? You say you did not like being a slave, but didn't you have slaves in your Gallia?"

"No, we usually killed captured men, if we could not get ransom money for them," Seamus answered. "Not just killed; we sacrificed them to our gods,"

"See?" Alexius said, "You sacrificed live people to your pagan gods! Is not that terrible? And if you hadn't been brought to Rome, you would still do that! Could that be the very lesson you were brought here for?"

"But I learned this lesson!" Seamus proudly raised his head and hit his chest with his fist. "I will never serve other gods and never make sacrifices to them. I learned, and I am still here. Why? There is only one explanation – I must still do something else, now and here. And I know what it is!"

"Did you? Did you really learn?" Alexius fixed his cool eyes on the barbarian. "You say you've learned not to kill, but what is it you are trying to do now? Burn Rome? How many people will die in the flames?"

"That's different," Seamus said. "I won't kill them, the flames will. The flames will clean up the place and separate good from evil!"

"Separate, you say?" Alexis asked. "How interesting. It reminds me of your friend Hosta. I heard he was sent to the countryside for his rebellious temper? What is he doing there?"

"He is a shepherd now," Seamus said. "Why?"

"And what does he do when some of his sheep get sick?"

"I guess he first separates them from the healthy sheep, so that the rest of the herd does not gets sick," Seamus answered. "Then he tends to them. And if he fails, he kills them. Because one bad sheep can spoil the whole herd; better for one sheep to die than the whole herd to perish. That's exactly what we should do with Rome, because Romans are bad sheep."

"Separates, you say? Bad sheep from good ones, you say? Sick from healthy?" Alexius paused and looked around. "You know who else is doing this job?"

Now all eyes were on the old man. Seconds passed in silence. "Who? Who?" the people in the crowd shouted.

"The devil!" Alexius said loudly and looked around at the shocked eyes. "Don't you remember? He was an angel and God's servant, but he did not trust Him and he did not like people. He rebelled, just like Seamus' friend. Did he succeed? Of course not! How could he succeed against our Lord, the God Almighty? He is still God's servant and does His bidding. Do you know which job he was assigned after the rebellion? He has the same job as Seamus' friend – separating the bad sheep from the good, so that our Lord can tend to the sick separately."

"But, Alexius," a muscular, dark-haired man behind Seamus said, "does not the devil rule hell, where souls are tortured?"

"And, what do you think hell is," Alexius said, "if not the place where sick souls can be isolated and tended to separately?"

"But they are tortured there, not tended!" the man answered.

"You, Hludwick, you took an arrow in your leg in one of your battles," Alexius said. "What did you feel when *medicus* took it out?"

"Pain, what else?" Hludwick answered.

"So, when your leg is treated you expect pain. Would not it be even more painful when something as important as the soul is treated? What is hell if not the place where sick souls are tended and cured from cruelty and godlessness? When the devil tempts people, he is only looking to separate the bad sheep from the good." Alexius turned from the crowd and stared into his opponent's eyes. "Why do you want to do the devil's job, Seamus?"

"Don't talk to me like that, Alexius! You will not confuse me with your rhetoric. You Greeks are cowards! You are born slaves and you remain slaves all your lives. You allow the cruel scoundrel who rules the empire to do whatever he wants! But I was born free! I was born to fight, and I will fight in the name of our Lord!"

"Why would I fight?" Alexius asked. "God sent me here, and He certainly had a plan for that. He sent us many things – Rome, the empire, and the emperor among others. Good or bad, that's all part of his plan. If he sent the emperor to rule us, then he had a reason. Why would I fight against His plan?"

"He did this so we can show our faith in Him and fight injustice," Seamus answered. "You are too afraid to fight, but what will you do? Go to your precious emperor and give us up to him?"

The crowd got silent for a few moments. Then a man behind Alexius cut through the tension and said, "Don't be ridiculous, Seamus. You know we cannot betray our brothers."

"But we will beg you to change your mind," Alexius said. "If you succeed, or even if you are caught trying, think what it will bring to all of us. They will blame all Christians for what you will try to do. They will hunt us down like animals. Aren't our lives hard enough already?"

"So, you are afraid. As I said, you are cowards!" Seamus grinned with satisfaction and turned away. "We will do this for you, you cowards! We will do our part, and yours as well, timid brothers. We'll save you from the empire, whether you want it or not, even if we have to die doing it. Just don't interfere." Seamus suddenly disappeared into the darkness and a dozen of his loyal supporters followed him.

The silence was broken only by the sounds of receding footsteps. Then someone asked, "What can we do now?"

"The Lord has the sick sheep separated," Alexius said looking into the dark shadows where Seamus and his men disappeared. Then he looked around at the people who surrounded him, waiting eagerly for his quiet voice to continue. "Now let us pray to our Lord to save his good sheep."

CAN WE BURN HIS HOUSE, PLEASE?
Chapter IV, where doctor Noot gets a bit more than he had asked for

Rome's streets in the daytime are full of people, noise, and dirt. In fact, they are full of dirt any time of the day. And it's easy to get pushed into it unless you are strong enough to push everybody out of your way, or wealthy enough to have a strong slave who will do that for you. However, if you are wealthy, you are better off using a horse or a palanquin carried by slaves rather than mingling with plebs. That's not fun. Seriously.

On the Day of Rest, an aged man walked through the streets of Rome in the direction of Palatine hill. He did not use a horse, although he was apparently wealthy enough to have a strong slave. His slave – a tall, dark-haired Gaul, with strong muscles and an impressive torso showing under a simple tunic – was probably a prisoner of one of the small border wars with Gaul and German tribes on the far northwest corner of the empire, who was sold into slavery. To give him credit, he did his job very well, pushing other pedestrians out of his master's way. He carried in his left hand a pair of sandals and an old, small, wooden chest that looked like the work of old Egyptian artisans. The master himself was dressed in a white Greek *chlamys* on top of a regular light-brown Roman tunic, and soft leather *calcei* shoes, pretty common for outdoor use. However, anybody who looked at his light brown face, and the piece of fabric covering his hair in Egyptian style, could guess his origin was from the land of Osiris.

Doctor Nut'anh, whom Roman barbarians called simply Doctor Noot, was an expert in what we now call dentistry. After learning his profession in his home city of Alexandria, he moved to Rome, where there was less competition and more wealthy patients to tend to. At this time, he had already lived in the Eternal City for more than three dozens years and had a great success with the city's privileged and wealthy elite. In fact, right now he was going to one of those wealthy and influential patients. This time a bit too influential for his taste, but he hoped to turn this fact to his own benefit, as the prefect of Praetorian Guards could be useful on the very complicated and delicate problem that Doctor Noot had on his hands.

Doctor Noot was the head of the Roman Dental and Plumbing Association, or simply a Lead Guild, so called because its members extracted most of their profit from the trade secrets of working with lead, a very soft and easy to shape metal used for water pipes and dental fillings. The trouble started with a disagreement between Jewish and Egyptian factions of the guild. One of the prominent members of a Jewish faction, Doctor ben Ata Khin, suggested that lead may actually be harmful to humans and hence should not be used in dental fillings. As an alternative, he suggested the use of gold or ivory instead of lead.

It's absolutely ridiculous, thought Doctor Noot, lead was used for years without any visible consequences! Although it seems that my esteemed colleague just found a new way to charge customers more. In fact, that's a splendid idea. If not for...

Yes, Doctor Noot would support it with all his heart if not for two problems. First, many younger members of the guild had not yet established a clientele rich enough to afford gold and ivory fillings. That was not acceptable because the guild had to support its younger members if it wanted to exist in the future. The second problem was that another huge source of income for guild members was coming from making, fixing, and installing lead water pipes for the city. Admitting that lead is dangerous would require using some other material for these pipes, and there was none. Clearly, gold and ivory could not be used for plumbing.

These arguments did not stop the Jewish faction from pushing their point of view. After all, most of the Jewish members were dentists and not plumbers; hence, the second problem did not concern them. As to the first problem, it would allow them to keep the younger members of the guild as their low-paid assistants for quite a bit, so it was not so bad for them either.

Doctor Noot was a seasoned expert in internal politics and had a lot of experience handling internal guild conflicts. Hence, after a series of conversations, most of the Jewish members agreed to abstain from doing anything drastic and stand aside, waiting for the issue to resolve. However, a small group, led by Doctor ben Ata, started an aggressive propaganda campaign against the use of lead, and many of Doctor Noot's customers started to ask unpleasant and, in Doctor Noot's opinion, quite stupid questions. Not that he did not enjoy charging them for gold and ivory fillings, not at all, but still it was a problem.

When Doctor Noot came to the place, an elderly slave met him at the door, apparently waiting for his arrival. He was dressed in a simple off-white tunic, but had a majestic mane of gray hair and a certain dignity that only old trusted servants can emanate. He waited until the doctor changed from shoes to sandals, and then showed him and his servant to the small garden in the internal yard that was surrounded by columns and passageways. The prefect, Ophonius Tigellinus, was lying on a couch, home-style, in a bright green tunic, with his face twisted in pain.

"Salve, Noot," the prefect said. "I already thought of sending a few guards after you just in case you faced some unexpected delays on the way to my home!"

"Salve, honorable Tigellinus!" Doctor Noot bent over with a slimy smile. He felt a momentary weakness in his legs, and his hands, pressed against his chest, started to shake against his will. He could easily recognize the hint of a threat, and he knew better than to underestimate it. Then he gathered himself and said, "It's always a high honor and pleasure to be of help to you!"

"I would not say it's a pleasure for me," Tigellinus said with a wry smile and pointed to a simple chair near the couch. "Sit here and see what you can do about this cursed tooth of mine."

Doctor Noot made a sign to his servant, and he put the chest on a small and low round table near the patient. Then the doctor sat on the chair as ordered and said, "Would you open your mouth so that I can see the problem?"

Tigellinus opened his mouth wide and for some time both went silent. The prefect hardly could say anything with a widely open mouth, and Doctor Noot was busy looking inside and figuring out the cause and the treatment. After a bit Tigellinus became bored, closed his mouth and asked, "Well?"

"You have a small hole in your third molar on the right, honorable Tigellinus," Doctor Noot said. "I could clean it up from decaying food, and then fill it up with a seal made of lead, gold, or ivory, as you prefer."

"And will it stop aching?"

"I will put in an extract of certain plants after cleaning. It will relieve you from the pain. And after the hole is filled up, it should stay well until the filling drops out, which should not be soon," said the doctor. "About materials – common folks use lead, but for a man of your position gold or ivory would, probably, be more appropriate."

"So be it, let's use the gold," Tigellinus said. "Besides, I've heard that lead may harm people. Is it true?"

"Absolutely not!" the doctor answered. "We, at Roman Dental and Plumbing Association, have used lead for years and nobody ever complained. Let me start the treatment. Meanwhile I'll tell you all you want to know about lead and these rumors."

Doctor Noot reached for the chest on the table, took out of it a couple of bronze needle-like tools, and once again bent over the opened mouth. He started to clean the crevice and continued. "You see, lead is a very soft and useful material. We used it to fill the teeth for years, and everybody was just fine. As you may know, we also use it for the water pipes. Following the same logic, all the Roman water should be poisonous, but is it? Not at all! It's clean and good. These rumors were started by this Judean doctor, ben Ata, just to frighten our customers. And he is completely wrong!"

Tigellinus indifferently listened to the doctor, allowing him to do his job.

"And he is completely irresponsible," Doctor Noot continued. "Imagine that his rumors about lead get to the people, and they start thinking that Roman water is poisonous? We could have a revolt on our hands just because of this crazy doctor and his bogus theories!"

Now Tigellinus waved a hand to the doctor to stop, and when he got out of his mouth asked, "So what do you want?"

"I am wondering," Doctor Noot asked, "if the authorities could take care of this doctor to avoid the public disturbances that he can bring?"

"No," Tigellinus said after a small pause. "You are right, his theories are dangerous. But if we execute him, more people will believe in his theories. Just handle him yourself."

"Oh, certainly, honorable Tigellinus," Doctor Noot said. "We actually thought about burning his house to the ground, but we were worried if praetorians and vigilantes would allow that. You know, we don't want to break the law. It's just as loyal, concerned subjects of the empire..." The doctor looked at the prefect expectantly, fearing that he asked for too much, and then added, "Could we burn ben-Ata's house, please?"

Tigellinus thought for a few seconds, then nodded affirmatively and said, "Yes, that would be all right. I suggest you do that on the third day of September Ides. I think both praetorians and vigilantes will be too busy that day to bother you, so you could do it without interference. If you have any trouble, demand to be brought to me. Of course, it's better if you do it unnoticed."

Tigellinus opened his mouth again. Doctor Noot made a sign, and the slave, who was attentively following the conversation, picked up two new tools from the chest and passed them to the doctor.

After the doctor did his work and left, Tigellinus lay down on the couch and thought. It's good that Noot and his men will take care of this crazy doctor. Among other affairs happening around, a revolt would be one of the last things that he would like to see. But what's more important, Tigellinus smiled at the thought, is that he had now the link to Egyptians and through them to Christians.

He was way more correct about the latter than he thought.

* * *

Late in the evening, when the darkness of the night covered the streets of the Eternal City, a tall muscular man snuck out of the house of Doctor Noot through the back door. It was Hludwick, the slave who accompanied the doctor this morning to the prefect's house. He walked in the same direction toward Palatine Hill as he did early that day when accompanying the doctor.

When he came close to the hill, he turned and found a narrow opening in the side of the hill between two buildings. He forced himself through it and entered the Roman catacombs. After moving by touch for about a hundred feet in the darkness, he turned left and got to an underground hall about twenty steps wide and long. Several poorly dressed people were sitting around a small fire that lit up the place and allowed them to see. Hludwick exchanged a few words with them, got a lit torch and moved forward into the deeper part of the old stone labyrinth. These tunnels were left in the base of the hill after limestone was mined here to build the palace above. In the light of the torch, gray stone walls looked crème with contrasting black spots of entrances to side passages here and there. After about a ten minute walk, one of the entrances to the left turned out to be lit from inside with the same live fire. Hludwick turned there and entered another small underground hall with several people and a fireplace. A light smoke from the fire was going up and disappearing in the cracks in the ceiling. One of the men sitting near the fire turned to the newcomer, showing a terrible scar on his face.

"Seamus," Hludwick said. "I have important news. I was in the house of the prefect of praetorians today with my master. I heard them speaking about the arson, which my master wants to do to his competitor. The prefect advised him on the day. On the third day of September Ides praetorians and vigilantes will be busy with something. It may be a very good time to implement your plan!"

Here, underground, below the palace of Tiberius, was the meeting place of Seamus' followers.

WE ARE HELPING THE EMPEROR, PACHO!
Chapter V, where Nil looks for a pleasure and finds a ship and information.

It was early evening when the paved road brought Nil to Tarentum. This former Greek town was once fighting Rome for its independence under the hand of the famous Greek King Pyrrhus. Now, it was living the life of a Roman provincial city and a major seaport. One- or two-story buildings, without trees or much of any other vegetation in front of them, surrounded the streets paved with cobblestone. Actually, there was vegetation inside, in the shadowy internal yards, but, like anything else, it was hidden behind stone walls built to provide privacy and seclusion.

Nil rode to the waterfront and stopped in front of a tavern facing Tarentum bay. It was a ramshackle two-story building with the dining room on the first floor and the guest rooms on the second. This tavern was not much better or worse than most others in the town. In fact, it was somewhat better than many others. Nil threw the reins of his horse into the hands of a slave boy, pushed the wooden door, darkened by the time, and entered. A barefoot *ancilla*, a slave girl, in a clean off-white tunic, showed him to the table in the better side of the tavern, where customers were reclining on couches, like in Rome, instead of sitting on stools or benches. Narrow purple stripes on his dress were the best pass to this part of the tavern as they gave away his equestrian rank. On another hand, his solemn manners, military clothes, and good fabric were as good signs to the experienced eye of the fat and garrulous *caupo* – innkeeper and bartender – who immediately popped up near the profitable customer. Hey, profitable or not, a man with solemn manners and military clothes could beat him without any repercussions, so it was wise to give him some immediate attention.

"What would you like, honorable citizen?" the innkeeper asked in the most flattering voice he could.

"Wine, cheese, bread, some meat," Nil said, "and a room for one for a few days, until I find a ship out of here. And I want everything edible on the list promptly!"

"Just a moment!" the innkeeper said, made a sign to the servant, and in less than a minute Nil really got his bread, cheese, and wine. The innkeeper said, almost apologizing, "The meat will require some time to be prepared, your honor, if it is ok."

"Sure, do it right," Nil answered. "As long as I have something on the plate, I'd rather have the main dish done right! After all, the emperor's orders don't include eating raw meat."

The innkeeper disappeared into the kitchen while Nil devoted his time to tasting the local red wine, traditionally mixed with water, and he found it pretty good.

Several men in the common part of the tavern attentively listened to this conversation. After it finished, the eldest one thought for a minute and then gave a solemn nod to the others. As if it started some mysterious, well-prepared plan, another man in the group called the ancilla, who served the tables, and carefully whispered several words to her. The girl looked at Nil and nodded as in agreement.

* * *

Life was good. Actually, the wine was good. Well, the meat was good too, and the goat cheese and bread were not bad either, but the wine was definitely superb. At least it was strong enough to feel that way. Hey, he was unlikely to sail off tomorrow anyway, especially so early in the spring. As he knew already, most of experienced seamen would not go to sea until May because of the storm season. So he relaxed and thought about how he could spend forced delay with the most pleasure or, at least, most comfort for himself. Besides, southern Italy was famous for its good wine and hospitality.

It looked like he found the place to sleep and the place where wine was not bad, so he was mostly ok. Next on the list was a woman. When he really gets to a ship, he will have dozens of days without a woman so it was only reasonable to think about this now.

His thoughts were interrupted by the ancilla who brought more wine and bread to his table. She bent over the table placing the plate and the wine pitcher. Her short tunic left the knees open and showed her body contours mere inches from his eyes. Nil grabbed the girl's petite hand, put his other hand on her back below the waist, and asked, "Would you come to my room later?"

"If my master will allow," said the girl and looked at the innkeeper, "I'd be glad to brighten your night in this place."

"I bet he will allow, for a few more coins!" Nil said with a laugh, pleased with his good luck. Just a woman was not a problem in any corner of the empire, but a relatively fresh and beautiful one? That was a nice hint from the fortune. After finishing laughing Nil said, "Get some wine and food to my room too, will you?"

The girl smiled with a promise to him and turned to serve other customers. Nil threw a few coins on the table for the innkeeper who immediately appeared as from nowhere. The coins immediately disappeared and his flattering smile indicated his readiness to serve an honorable customer and provide whatever Nil expressed his interest in.

After Nil ate, he stood up and demanded to show him to his room. The same girl appeared immediately and showed him the way. When they entered the room he found that his request was fulfilled; the wine, bread, and cheese were already in the room. He threw his cloak into the corner, sat on the couch and grabbed the girl. She sat on his knees for a few moments while he enjoyed the initial feel and touch, then got off and bent in front of him, unlacing his sandals.

"Would you like more wine?" she asked.

"Sure," Nil said with a merry laugh, "Both you and wine, and don't worry about the bread!"

The girl smiled, filled a bowl with wine and brought both requested items back to Nil. This night promised to be very pleasurable to Nil, but it was going to end sooner than he expected. After a few sips from the bowl, Nil felt that he really needed to lay back and sleep. The girl still looked very attractive but for some reason she could not compete with a call from Morpheus. So, surprised at himself, Nil fell asleep in mere minutes while trying to get his hands under the girl's tunic and take it off.

* * *

Waking up was much less pleasurable. The head was heavy and the eyes refused to look straight. Besides that, Nil felt that this was a different room, not the one where the girl led him. By the way, talking about the girl, the person standing in front of him was definitely not her. The guy was breathing into his face with a mixture of smells including onions, rotten teeth, and the cheap wine that Romans called *acetatum* for a reason.

"Huh, he is getting up, boss!" the man said and breathed into Nil's face a new wave of horrible smells.

"Stand aside, Pacho." Another voice came from the side. A short but stout man came to the light of a torch from behind, and Nil recognized him from the nearby table in the tavern. "His Honor just got too much wine, but he is now ready to tell us what he wants from us, poor Sicilian seamen."

"I want from you?" Nil asked and attempted to point his finger to the man's chest. "What the hell I would want from you, scum?"

"You told us, Your Honor," the man said, "that you have a matter of most importance entrusted to you by the emperor himself, and that you require our assistance."

The man had short gray hair and wore a dark cloak. His words were flattering, but his eyes stayed cold and strong. Nil liked these kinds of people, useful and capable. So he managed to concentrate, and thoughts started to brew in his mind that maybe this meeting was not an accident – maybe the gods were trying to help him? But what could he use these guys for? Could they know or have heard something? After all, it'll be weeks until he reaches Egypt, and what harm could happen if he questioned a few seamen before talking to the Egyptians? Probably none.

"What's your name, man?" Nil asked.

"Bokha, Your Honor, Bokha from Messina. You know, decent Sicilian folk, not some Greek scum from Syracuse," the man answered, "I am the captain of my own ship and I have a lot of friends in many ports across Italy, Sicily, and Africa."

"And why are you so polite and helpful, Bokha?" Nil asked. "Where is your money in that?"

"You see, Your Honor, I had a little trouble paying customs in the past," Bokha answered. "And guards were so helpful as to oversight this little incident with a condition that I should be helpful to the people like you."

"I see," Nil said and smiled. So he got a bona fide Sicilian pirate with a lot of connections who also worked for Tigellinus. That made a lot of sense now. Certainly the gods were favorable to him today, except for the episode with that too strong wine and the girl, of course. It would be a pity to miss the opportunity to question the guy. With his lifestyle, he would definitely hear about a lot of things happening around. "Tell me, Bokha, do you see a lot of Christians in your travels?"

"There are some around, Your Honor," Bokha said. "They are everywhere. Why do you ask?"

"You see, what I need from you is to think carefully and try to recall if you heard Christians talking about some disaster that's going to happen in Rome?"

"Yes, Your Honor, I definitely heard," the pirate smiled. "In fact, I've seen several Christians saying that Rome will be destroyed soon. Just a month ago, I met a Christian merchant who prophesied that Rome will see its end not further than this autumn."

"Prophesied?" Nil asked.

"Yes, Your Honor. They have these prophesies, they have a lot of prophesies, and they always argue about them between themselves."

"Do you think it could be not a prophesy, but something they will actually try to do?" Nil asked. "And, by the way, did he mention any particular day?"

Nil paused, looking straight at the pirate. Bokha thought for a few seconds, then his face started to show understanding and some recollection.

"Yes, Your Honor, I think he did plan something," he said. "His name was Benjamin, and he owned a load of oil that he was bringing to Rome to sell, or so he said. He came on a Greek ship from Achaia , but I think he is from Judea or Crete. As about the date, I think he did say something, but I don't recollect exactly. I think something in September." Well, thought Bokha, if this is autumn, how far from September could it be? "Could you remind me, what is the date you are talking about? Then I will be able to recall if it is the same date or not."

"How about the third day of September Ides?" Nil asked.

"Precisely! The third day of September Ides!" Bokha said and smiled again. "How could I forget? This merchant even explained that this is a good time because it's just days before the Ides, so the people coming to Rome for celebrations will be already in the city and so they will witness this too."

I'll be damned if he did, thought the pirate, but let this Benjamin prove opposite if they ever find him. At least, he noticed in his thoughts while continuing to smile, even if such guy exists, he could not recognize me, because I certainly never met him.

As to Nil, he had completely different thoughts now. What luck! He should immediately write a letter to Tigellinus. If they catch this Benjamin, his whole trip could be unnecessary! Of course, he will continue, but what great luck he had today.

"Thank you, Bokha. I'll tell some people in Rome how much you helped us," Nil said. "You may count on guards' lenience as long as you don't go over some reasonable limits, of course."

"What else can we do for you, Your Honor?" the pirate asked. "You know, we have a lot of strong men who can go to Rome and prevent this scum from doing whatever they plan to do."

"I think praetorians and vigilantes will handle that," Nil said. "If you happen to be in Rome that day, you'll see that yourself. But your attitude as a loyal subject of the empire is laudable. Now, it's time for me to depart. By the way, I believe you know everybody in the port, Bokha. Is there a ship that departs to Egypt or nearby soon?"

"Of course I know a lot of people around, Your Honor. As to the ship, it's a bad time now. Most ships are safely in the harbor waiting for the storm season to end. But I know a ship that goes to Judea with a stop on Crete in a few days. It's not as far to Egypt from there. The ship is called 'Glapos'. That means 'Seagull'. Its captain is nicknamed Glap after his ship. He is Greek and an old friend of mine. We had some business deals before," Bokha said, helping Nil get on his feet and showing him to the exit. "Just tell him my name and he will be very happy to take you aboard for a modest fee."

After Nil was gone, the second man started to look at Bokha with a puzzled expression on his face but clearly afraid to open his mouth.

"Yes, Pacho, I see that you are confused. What is it that you want to ask me?" the pirate said with all traces of sweet flattery gone from his face and voice.

"Yes, Bokha, I am confused. Why did we let him go? He has gold on him. When Lara put a sleeping potion into his wine, we wanted to question and kill him. The gold would be ours, and nobody could find out who did it, right?"

"Pacho, stupid Pacho," the pirate said with a soft fatherly voice, "You see why you should never question me and always do what I say?"

"Yes, boss, I always do what you say. You are the boss."

"Right, Pacho, I am the boss, and I am smart. I know what we are doing. I let him go so that he can take my words to Rome. And do you know why we want him to take my words to Rome?"

"Why, boss? So that he can catch that merchant with oil?"

"No, Pacho," Bokha said and sighed. "Because then after we–" Bokha paused for a moment stressing 'we', then continued, "–set a fire in Rome on that day, everybody will think that this merchant and Christians did it, and we will be heroes who warned in advance."

"Ugh-hm…" Pacho clearly wanted to ask more, but was afraid to.

"Why do we want that? For many reasons, Pacho. First, heroes are getting their merchandize oversighted by customs, and that's a very good reason. Second, guards will be busy, and so we won't have to worry about them in our business for some time. Third, we will avenge my brother. He was a decent man, and a few lousy payments are not a good reason to get him executed. And which house do you think will we set fire to first?" Bokha asked and raised his finger in front of Pacho's face. "This scoundrel Drákon from Syracuse is getting in our way too often lately. He's gone so far as to have his own warehouse in

Rome. He has there a lot of oil, and some other stuff, you know, but mostly really just a lot of oil. It will burn beautifully."

"You are so wise, Bokha!" Pacho said.

"Yes, I am, Pacho. Never doubt me," the pirate said. "And apart from these reasons, there is one more. It's clear that the emperor wants to get rid of these Christians, and it looks like he needs a reason. You see? We are helping the emperor, Pacho!"

* * *

After getting back to the tavern, Nil ordered more wine and food to his room. The girl was gone somewhere, but after all the events of the night he was not in a romantic mood anyway. Maybe tomorrow. So he asked the innkeeper for a stylus and a clean *tabula*, a waxed piece of wood used by Romans to write, and came to his room to write a message to the prefect. Tomorrow he will leave it with the local office and *cursus publicus* – the imperial post – will carry it over Appian Way back to Rome quickly and confidentially into the hands of Tigellinus.

The oil lamp gave enough light to write and Nil started. After the greeting lines he paused for a moment, thinking how to write it, and then scribed on the tablet:

"…the Sicilian pirate and the captain of his own vessel, Bokha from Messina, just informed me that a month ago he met a merchant named Benjamin who had a load of oil to sell in Rome. Bokha said that this merchant is Christian, from Crete or Judea, and that he came on a Greek ship from Achaia. Bokha said that this merchant told him about some rebellious acts that the Christians plan for the third day of September Ides just like you suspected…"

JUST IN CASE
Chapter VI, where Nil gets a new name and a death sentence in absentia

Palatine Hill is busy in nighttime, but the mornings... well, that's a completely different story. Oh, sure, there is always somebody around, it's just not the splendor of the nights. In the nighttime there is a lot of guests, and every guest tries to do his best. The best clothes, the best hairstyle, the best jewelry, the best women. Especially like the last night with the great reception to celebrate Veneralia, the festival in honor of Venus, the goddess of love...

The large reception hall have been full of jesters, politicians, imperial court freeloaders, and other parasites. Not that anybody cares to distinguish one kind from another. Not a lot of white clothes today; that's not the goddess's favorite color. Bright green, blue, and yellow togas color the place. Tunics are still white. Well, you want your purple stripes, showing your senator or equestrian rank, to be visible in the palace. Not that they matter as much these days in Rome as they have before, but there is still a lot of power behind them. An abundance of oil lanterns and candles of the best beeswax lighten up the place. No smoky torches for the emperor, but the doors to the garden are still opened a bit to let the fresh air in. And between small talk, doublespeak, evocative hints, and occasional blunders, everybody hails Venus for most of the night with a great help from the god of wine Bacchus, who is not neglected either.

The mornings are different. Accidental people are gone, jesters too, even politicians are not here, except for the most persistent ones. Nights are for the public – selected elite public. But mornings are shared with your own kind.

The emperor made an effort and opened his eyes. The sight was not soothing at all. He'd rather see that girl from last night. He could not remember her name, but who cares? It certainly would be better than what he saw now, which was Tigellinus who was equally struggling to keep his eyes open.

"Butler!" the emperor almost whined. The sound of his own voice resonated all over his body, and especially his head. Anyway, the result was achieved and the butler appeared almost immediately.

"Good," the emperor said, "bring me and the prefect that Hyperborean morning drink of salted cucumber juice."

It was already several months since he switched to this strange drink as a cure for morning hangover. Some of the palace courtiers brought in the recipe claiming it to be an invention of Hyperborean people, the people populating the mysterious northern land that nobody had really seen but many had heard about. Many suspected that it did not even exist and, frankly, there was not much evidence to prove otherwise. Real or not, nobody cared. Too far, too North, too cold, and the empire had better things to worry about.

Anyway, the drink was real, and it was helping a lot. The emperor drank a few deep long gulps of the invigorating liquid and began to feel much better. Now he could turn his head and move his eyes. With some surprise, he noticed that the girl was nearby all the time, still mostly naked and sleeping mere inches from him. For a few moments, he was puzzled by the question of what she was doing around him shortly before he blacked out. Keeping in mind the amount he drank, she was hardly of any use to him at that time. The thoughts were moving in his head slowly, like an old cart squealing and squeaking on a narrow and empty street. Wait, the squeaking was not exactly in the head, it was in the right ear. He turned the head to the left; yes, definitely in the right ear.

While the emperor enjoyed introspection, Tigellinus drank some of the liquid too and was now able to move. The large hall was mostly clean. In a few hours, servants cleaned up the tables and floors, carefully arranged the guests who dropped into sleep right at the table, put out the candles and lanterns, and now only the gloomy daylight coming from the garden doors lit up the place. Both men stood up and slowly walked through them outside. The fresh cold spring air revived both a bit.

"You know," the emperor said, "I never get why nobody follows up the compliments that Petronius gives me. When you praise me there is always somebody who cheers up and shouts 'Right!' But not with Petronius. Why?"

"They probably think that he will get even more influence on you if they join his compliments," Tigellinus answered. "Why does it bother you?"

"Not bother, just puzzles," the emperor said. "Remember, yesterday he said that my voice is so strong that people in Greece could enjoy my singing. Pretty elegant, isn't it? By the way, about the games. Do you think the public applauded me sincerely enough?"

"They'd better." The prefect attempted to chuckle, but hangover struck him again.

"Dirty pigs! They don't appreciate my talent," the emperor complained. "I have to waste my talent on dirty stupid pigs who populate this city."

"True, Caesar," Tigellinus said. "They don't deserve your talent. They don't deserve to live in this city."

"And speaking of the city," the emperor continued, "what do we have around? Here on Palatine everything is beautiful and nice, but go down to areas populated by plebs, and what do you see? Dirty narrow streets, stinking air, utilitarian brick and wood boxes filled with creatures who gorge, copulate, and produce even more stink. I hate this city. How beautiful I could make it if I could build it on an empty place."

"Well, nothing is lost yet," Tigellinus said.

"What do you mean?" the emperor asked.

"You know, those Christians we talked about before. I have reliable data that they are going to set a massive fire in the city."

"What data?"

"Well, I have one Egyptian doctor," Tigellinus said, "who will try to set fire to the house of his Jewish colleague."

A qualm distracted the emperor for a moment, but then the prefect's words started to seep in. He looked at Tigellinus with a puzzled expression.

"Ophonius, you said 'Christians', right?"

"Yes, you see, Christians are Jews, so we have a Jew, and they never broke their connections with Egypt, and we have an Egyptian..." Tigellinus broke off.

The emperor gave him a frown, then closed his eyes, put his hands on his temples, and quietly whined.

"Not good, right?" Tigellinus asked.

"No, not good at all," the emperor said. "You need to have something more convincing for the Romans to put the blame on the Christians. And, if you forgot, they have to really burn Rome first to put the blame on them."

"Don't worry about that," Tigellinus said. "I've already sent a man to Egypt–"

"To do what? Put the blame on Christians?"

"Kind of."

"Ophonius, what the hell are you doing?" The emperor turned to the prefect with a face wry of hangover headache. "First you say that some sect is trying to burn Rome. Fine, nothing new. Then you say that they may succeed, right? And now I hear that one of your men is in the middle of all of that? Do you want the people on the streets to think that I did it?"

"How will they know that he is one of our men?" Tigellinus asked. "He is on the mission, undercover."

"Look, I don't want to know what he is doing," the emperor said. "Just do the right thing. And remember, I'd like to rebuild the city if our enemies burn it. But I will not burn it myself! And I don't want you or any of your people to try it. I prohibit that. Do you understand me clearly?"

"Yes, Caesar! Absolutely clear," Tigellinus said, hiding a derisive smile under the mask of diligence.

"And if this man's cover blows up, I want to be sure that nobody tries to blame me or you. Is that clear?" The emperor paused until Tigellinus gave him a nod. "Now, what can we do?"

"Can we say that he is a traitor?"

"Not bad," the emperor said. "But what about the Christians? I guess your guy has a Roman name, right? Who will believe that he is a Christian?"

"Right," Tigellinus agreed. "Let's give him a new name. I have a Jewish slave in my house. He cleans the toilets, but otherwise he is quite a bright boy. He says that their names start from 'ben', which means 'son of'. Say, son of a man named Titus will be 'ben Titus.' How about 'ben Nihil'?"

"Son of Nothing? Is it a joke? Anyway, still too Roman." The emperor snorted, thought for a few seconds, and then asked, "What is the name of this slave of yours?"

"Benjamin."

"Ben Jámen? Not bad," the emperor said. "Let's call him ben Jamen from now on. That sounds Jewish enough and it will be easy to present as a Christian name."

"Sure thing," Tigellinus said. "So, from now on the former Praetorian Guard and traitor, a Christian by the name ben Jamen, is going to be the leader of the scoundrels who are going to burn Rome."

"I still hope he does not," the emperor said. "Don't forget, that's just in case his cover blows up. You know what? Maybe we should put him on a post scriptum list. You know, just in case. That makes a lot of sense. We found out he is a traitor and gave him a death sentence. Too bad he escaped, but we did our part, right? That would cover our story just fine."

"Consider it done, Caesar," Tigellinus said.

SURE THING, GLAP
Chapter VII, where we learn that there is a lot to loot in Rome and that Drakon knows how to be grateful

Nil had very little difficulty finding Captain Glap and his ship in the port. His ship, *Glapos*, was a galley of a popular *penteconter* type with 50 oars, a single rowing deck, a rectangular sail on a single mast, and command decks at the stern and bow. Several centuries ago it was a popular type of warship, but now powerful triremes and maneuverable Liburnian galleys ruled the seas. That's not to mention that all the major fleets were enforced with heavy *quadriremes* and *quinqueremes*. *Glapos* was still mighty enough to deal with a light pirate or trade vessel, whether defending itself against it or the other way around.

The captain was a stout, bearded Greek in a dark brown wool hooded cloak on top of a light brown tunic. The tunic was embroidered around the neck but otherwise was really simple. The only piece of jewelry on him was a gorgeous belt and a long knife with an engraved sheath and a hilt decorated with a gem. Although it did not look like just a piece of jewelry on this man.

After Bokha was mentioned, the captain immediately agreed to take the passenger for a "reasonable" price. From the price he named, Nil guessed that the "dear business associate" Bokha was hardly the best friend of Glap, so it took a couple of hours in the nearby tavern to negotiate a truly reasonable price and get the deal. There was still a few days until the departure, both men had nothing else to do, so negotiations slid effortlessly into the celebration of the deal, which required more wine and then, of course, girls. Captain Glap knew the right girls around with the right kind of wine, so the three days until sailing off passed quite smoothly for Nil and completely according to his original plans.

* * *

Nil was not susceptible to sea sickness so he felt well and had a good appetite, but day after day with nothing to do started to get to him at last. He tried to sleep a lot, but you can only sleep so much. The captain was kind enough to invite Nil every night to share a bottle of wine with him and his mate, a stocky Greek from Epirus, who was named after some ancient politician and now abbreviated to simply Phocles. But again, a couple of hours listening to the captain's stories about himself and his ship are only two hours. For the rest of the time, Nil had to loaf on one of the two command decks, looking overboard at the infinite mass of water, sometimes blue, but most of the time gray because of the clouds hiding the sun. The storm season was not completely finished yet, and although they did not encounter any serious calamity, the weather was not fun.

On the tenth day, he was still looking overboard at the gray water that stretched to the horizon when he heard some noise on the rowing deck. The captain's mate, Phocles, was whipping a slave with Captain Glap supervising. Nil got down to them, considering the spectacle and a talk to be a great improvement over fruitless staring at the empty sea. The rowing deck was filled with benches for oarsmen with a wide space between them, which is where the action took place.

"See?" the captain said. "I'll never buy a Hyperborean slave again in my life. All they think about is how to run away. Can you imagine? He tried to escape in the middle of the sea! What a moron."

"Is that what he is punished for?" Nil asked.

"Nah... I don't like slaves who want to run away, but an idiot who runs to drown is a good warning for the rest. Look at what he did to the perfectly good oar!" Glap pointed to the end of an oar that looked like a family of beavers had some fun with it. "That's what he is whipped for. Now I have to replace the oar! I wonder how he did it? He had nothing, no knife, no file, no nothing, except the iron chain that kept him in the place. Did he gnaw at it with his teeth?"

"It's good that he was chained," Nil said. "Seems like he could gnaw through ropes easily."

"Sure," Glap agreed. "Ropes don't work anyway. They rot quickly. The chains are more expensive, but also more practical, 'cause you don't have to change them every month or two."

"How did it happen that nobody noticed what he was doing?" Nil asked. "Looks like he spent a lot of time working on it."

"He was bending over it all the time, the son of a bitch! We would not have noticed if not for these two." Glap nodded in the direction of two galley-slaves who sat chained to the oars right behind the damaged one. "They are Christians, their faith tells them to be loyal to their master no matter who he is. So they gave up the stinker."

"Christians?" Nil asked. "I've never heard of a Christian doing something like that. Who are they?"

"Who knows? Bah! And who cares?" Glap laughed and made the sign to his mate to stop whipping. "They say they were sold to slavery because they were Christians. But the former owner said they became slaves by doing some dirty work in Rome."

"Christians doing dirty work," Nil said. "How interesting. Never heard of that. Can I talk to them?"

"Sure," Glap said and turned to the slaves in question. "Hey, dead meat! Honorable Nil wants to talk to you, scum. Answer him as you would answer me."

Both of them were tall and strong men with dark curly hair, naked like the rest of galley-slaves on other benches. As Nil could easily see, they were not Jewish. Probably from Greece, the Greek colonies or southern Italy. Or Rome, thought Nil, Rome gathered so many different people that almost anybody could be from Rome, from a fair-haired German to a dark-skinned Nubian. They were in their late twenties with scars from a whip on their backs, but none from a sword or any other weapon. Wait, the straight narrow scar on the left arm of the older one looked like it was inflicted with a knife. Thieves, maybe, Nil thought, robbers – unlikely, and not usual Christians for sure. Nil worked enough with this sect to recognize the peaceful, somewhat sheepish expression they carried on their faces. These were not sheep, but wolves. No, not wolves, jackals more likely. These could burn Rome. Or they could know someone who will.

"So, you say your faith demands you to answer honestly, right?" Nil asked.

"Yes, master," the older one said.

"Did you hear any of your Christian brethren talking about some disaster that's going to strike Rome? I mean the actual city?"

"Yes, master," the slave said. "Many people say that Rome is evil and going to be destroyed soon."

"How soon?" Nil asked.

"People do not agree on that," the slave said. "Some say in a few years, some say in a few months. You know, there is a prophesy that when Rome falls, good times will start. So some people are quite eager to see that, and some foretell it to happen as soon as this year."

"And could some of them take a part in making it happen this soon?" Nil asked.

"Not many, master," the slave said, "but some could. Are you asking about something in particular?"

"Yes, very particular," Nil said. "Did you hear anything about anybody planning to burn or attack Rome in some other way this Autumn?"

"I could've," the slave said after a pause. "Can I ask the kind master, will there be a reward in the event that I can recall that? Life on the galley is tough on my memory, it will be hard to recall–"

"I'll give you a reward, you scum!" Glap, visibly interested in the matter, interrupted and made a sign to his mate. "You will answer all the questions as asked, you understand? Or you will be whipped until you answer!"

Together with a slave driver, the mate took the man and put him face down on the deck. He raised the whip but the man started to cry:

"I remember! I'll tell, I'll tell everything I know!"

"Who was the man you are talking about?" Nil asked.

"I don't know his name. He was some Jew, they always prophesy the end of the world! Honestly, I don't know!"

"Could you just have forgotten? If you talked to him, what did you call him?"

"I don't remember, good master! Please, don't punish me more. It was one of their odd names, I don't remember," the slave said.

"Could it be Benjamin?" Nil suggested, remembering the story told by Bokha.

"Yes, yes, good master! Benjamin! Exactly that! Thank you, thank you! He was Benjamin, now I remember for sure."

"And when did they plan to do it?" Nil asked.

"I don't know the date. They said it like it was a prophesy." The whip hissed in the air.

"Sometime in the autumn, good master," the slave shouted. "Please don't whip me, I'll tell everything I know! I really will tell everything. Please, please, don't whip me!"

"So you say you don't know the day?" Nil asked with a grin on his face.

"I don't, good master, I really don't know. Please, don't hurt me–"

The whip struck the back of the man, leaving a red stripe on it.

"A-a-ah! Please, don't hurt me! Please, good master..."

"Don't cover your friends, scum," Glap said and turned to Nil. "He knows, he definitely knows, I can see it. Ask him harder, he will tell."

"You heard your master," Nil said. "Tell me, when will they try to burn Rome? I know they will. You cannot hide it from me. When?"

"I don't know, good master. Maybe September? October?"

Nil made a sign to Phocles and he raised the hand with a whip.

"September, good master, definitely September," the slave said.

"Somewhere around September Ides?" Nil asked cautiously.

"Yes, good master, yes, now I recall, around September Ides. Just like you said. You see, I am telling, I am telling everything!"

"What day? Which day of September Ides?" Nil asked.

"I don't remember, good master. Fifth? Ninth? Third?"

"You said 'third'?" Nil asked with a smile.

"Yes, good master, the third! Now I remember exactly, the third!"

Nil turned to Glap and waived a hand.

"Thank you, Captain. I think I've got everything I need to know from him."

While Phocles and the slave driver put the man back to the oar, Nil and the captain got to the upper deck.

"Glap, thanks for your help. By the way, keep what you've heard today quiet," Nil said. "You know, imperial affairs…"

"Sure thing, you can trust me on that," the captain said. "With such matters, the shorter tongue is good for the longer life. Sounds like trouble, eh?"

"Not if I can help it," Nil said.

* * *

Later in the night, two Greek slaves were whispering among themselves.

"Phaon," the younger slave said.

"What?" the older one asked

"Why did you say we are Christians?" the younger one asked.

"Would you prefer to tell the cap the real story?"

"Does it matter?"

"No, it does not," the older one said, "if we can escape and keep ourselves free."

"You got into trouble today because of it."

"Some crying and just one whip, nah, Phaos. Not much trouble," Phaon said. "But look what we've got for that."

"What?"

"Did you hear what that man said?" Phaon asked. "On the third day of September Ides there is going to be a large fire in Rome. Really large, if this guy is right."

"So, what? I don't care, let the Romans think about Rome," Phaos said.

"Little brother, you are missing the whole point," Phaon said with a chuckle. "Fire means disorder, confusion, mess. A large fire means a lot of disorder and mess. Including disorder in official records. After the fire happens, you and me will go around covered with soot and crying that our house and papers are gone. See? We can be free again."

"Only if you can bribe an official, old brother," Phaos said with a skeptical smile.

"Sure," Phaon agreed. "And who do you think will do some looting while the city is on fire? That's Rome, brother – there is a lot to steal there."

"I still see a little problem with your plan," Phaos said and clanked the chain that linked him to the oar.

"I saved the file that the barbarian used," Phaon said and nodded ahead to where the Hyperborean slave was sleeping, leaned against the oar. "It's made of very good iron and I think it can cut through the chains as well as it did with the wood. It's pretty cheap iron on the chains, it's narrow and soft. So in the nearest port we'll be gone."

* * *

About the same time on the main deck, the captain and his mate had a talk.

"Phocles, about the crap you've heard today. Keep it quiet," the captain said.

"Sure thing," the mate agreed. "You know, I am not a blab. But I think one man ought to know about it."

"Who?"

"Drakon," Phocles said. "He'd love to know when he could burn Bokha's store in Rome without much of a risk. And he knows how to be grateful."

"Not much love for our friend Bokha, huh?" Glap chuckled, thought for a moment, and then said, "You are right, let's let him know. But other than that, not to a single soul, Phocles, you understand?"

"Sure thing, Glap."

* * *

Three days later, when they almost reached their destination and the shore was already visible, a real storm came. It was still too far to reach a port or even find some bay to hide from the waves. The crew took the sail off and removed the mast, but despite all the hard work of oarsmen, the ship, driven by wind and waves, was moving slowly toward the shore.

On the positive side, the shore consisted mostly of sandy beaches, only rarely interrupted with rocky capes. When it became obvious that they could not win, Captain Glap made a decision to beach the ship on a wide sandy place in the hope that it would not result in much damage and may be set afloat again after the storm was gone.

Oarsmen turned the ship with the stern to the shore and thrust it backward. The ship ran aground on the sandy shoal a hundred steps from the dry place. Its sharp narrow bow was facing the waves coming on it from the open sea.

No one got injured, except three slaves at the oars who were washed away at the very last moment when the ship hit the bank. It looked like the chains broke, unable to resist the energy of waves. Nobody found it strange that all three were sitting next to each other. After all, when a wave hits, it does it most strongly in just one place. Nobody looked carefully at how the chains were broken. Nobody wondered what happened to these slaves, everybody thought they were gone and dead. Incidentally, these were the two Greek brothers and the Hyperborean.

IF WE ARE FAITHFUL ENOUGH
Chapter VIII, where Nil meets a clever zealot and the zealot meets a stupid Roman

Galleys were essentially large boats. They did not have a keel, so beaching was much safer for them than for later ships yet to come in future centuries, at least if they are really put firmly aground and not thrown around by the waves. Captain Glap's ship *Glapos* was firmly aground, so, except for a few broken oars and three missing slaves, it did not sustain any serious damage. Of course, it's bottom had to be tarred soon again, but that was pretty much it.

Still, the captain had to wait until the weather got better before attempting to get it afloat again. Fifty oarsmen and the crew could provide enough horsepower to move the ship even if it is completely beached – galleys were light – but not during the storm. So the only thing Glap could do for now was to curse and wait. According to the captain, they were a bit to the north and really close to Caesarea – a Roman port in Judea less than a day from the Jerusalem. Nil considered going to Jerusalem before Egypt because he suspected that local authorities, especially the Roman procurator of Judea, might have some valuable information on the subject. So Nil waited until the morning light broke, said thanks to the captain and his mate, wished them good luck, and got on the deserted road along the shore.

The road was local and quite poor, but the important thing about roads is that they almost always go from one place where people live to another. This was what Nil was looking for – a place where people live and where he could get a horse and directions. He knew that these areas are much less hospitable to a lonely wayfarer than the well guarded and patrolled Via Appia, but he had some military training and experience and he was sure that he could handle a bunch of peasants who decided to try their luck on a highroad.

Before he got to a place where people lived, he met some people traveling in the other direction. A crowd of poorly dressed men, many with staves in their hands, were coming toward Nil, crying something in the local tongue, chanting, gesticulating, and showing other signs of vivid communication. Some of them were in ragged and patched rubbish that was probably a tunic-like dress sometime in the past. Others wore a simple loin-cloth. Many of them wore simple sandals made of a sole and a couple of straps to keep it on the foot, but some just wrapped their foot in a piece of sheepskin. That's, of course, not to mention the few who were barefoot.

When the crowd and Nil met, people started to whisper some word in the local language, looking at Nil and pointing fingers at him. They were giving Nil the way with fearful covert glances at him. The whispers were getting louder and louder, until someone cried out something like "Ragal!" and the crowd attacked. Nil had military experience, so he crushed several jaws before he was overwhelmed by the mass. At some moment, somebody struck him on the head and Nil blacked out.

* * *

He regained consciousness in a small cave with an opening in the top. It was one of those caves that rains had washed out over centuries in the dull orange coarse-grained sandstone. There was only one man nearby and he was dressed completely differently than the road gang that attacked Nil. He was dressed in a Greek *himation*, somewhat similar to the Roman toga, on top of a *chiton*, both with embroidery. His feet were comfortably fit in a pair of good Roman-style sandals.

"Do you hear me?" he asked.

"Yeah..." Nil said. His head was heavy and he felt sick, besides, he had blood on the top of his head. Not enough to worry about, but it was not pleasant either. "And who are you?"

"My name is Temah the Samaritan, your honor. You see, I am a trader from the city of Samaria, which you call Sebaste," the man said. "I was traveling by the road and saw you lying with a wound on your head. I took you to this place to hide you from the sun and waited for you to awaken. I trade with Romans so I know your tongue. Take some water, your honor, you need it," the man gave Nil a cup with water.

Nil drank most of the water then soaked the edge of his cloak in the rest and wiped his face. Then he checked his possessions – no, nothing was gone, not even money. Those vagabonds were clearly not robbers. He touched the wound and winced in pain.

"Dirty sons of hyenas," he said. "They'll pay for this, if I can find them."

"Who do you think did this to you?" Temah asked.

"How do I know? Some crowd of dirty beggars, filthy and dirty," Nil said. "They were stepping aside and clearly feared me, so I did not expect them to attack. And then they cried something in local tongue like 'Ragal' and went on me."

"Tsk-tsk-tsk," Temah said. "'Ragal' means 'spy' in our language. Could it be because of your mission, you honor? You know, it's none of my business, but I saw that they did not even rob you."

Nil thought for a moment and it did not make any sense to him. Then he recalled the men who attacked him and said, "No, they don't look like Christians."

"Christians, you said?" Temah asked. "Tsk-tsk-tsk, oh my, you said they looked like beggars? That's very much like them. We good Jews don't like Christians. They are traitors. And you know, they hate Romans."

"And you 'Good Jews' like Romans, right?" Nil chuckled and winced in pain again.

"Not much, I admit," Temah said. "Some of us want to be free, that's true. Who doesn't, your honor? But we like to trade with you very much. Rome is rich and buys a lot."

"Free from Rome? So you would prefer to bow to Parthians?"

"Oh, no, not the Parthians, for God sake," Temah said. "Just free on our own. But we don't hate Rome, oh, no. Not like those Christians."

Something turned on in Nil's head. This guy talks a lot about Christians, he thought, and he hates them, and clearly he's met a lot of them.

"You say Christians hate Rome?" Nil asked. "Is it just hate or something more solid?"

"Everybody knows that they predict very bad things happening to Rome," Temah said. "And really soon."

"Looks like everybody does," Nil said with a wry smile. "Do you think they seriously plan to do these 'bad things' to Rome?"

"Sure, I can easily believe that," Temah said. "I apologize for asking you, your honor, but do you mean something solid?"

What the hell, Nil thought, it seems like everybody knows about it anyway except the imperial security.

"Did you hear of Christians planning to burn Rome on the third day of September Ides or some other day?"

Temah kept a silence for a few moments, then said, "Yes, your honor, I think I did. Not about burning Rome, but about something big and dramatic for sure. The man was not specific about what exactly will happen, he was more interested in the end of the world to follow. And I think he mentioned the date, although I thought that's just one of their stupid prophecies."

Nil sighed. It seemed like everybody really knew about that plan and had met this Benjamin at one time or another. This wasn't even amazing anymore. Then doubt came after him. This Benjamin seemed to be too omnipresent for a mere mortal. May it be several different men? It's hard to imagine such plans would be born independently at the same time, but even one plan may involve many people. If it was somebody else, it would be great to know about another conspirator in that group.

"Was his name by any chance Benjamin or was it some other name?" Nil asked.

"I think his name was Benjamin," Temah said. Who cares, he thought, what the name of this character is. "He is one of these traitors, you know, Christians. He deals with Greeks a lot, and nothing good comes from Greeks. Well, it's getting late, your honor. Can I help you get to your feet? I have a servant with me and an extra mule to spare. I am going to Caesarea and you are welcome to join me."

"Yes, thank you good Temah the Samaritan."

Nil sighed. Apparently, he heard again about that mysterious one and the only Benjamin. Anyway, getting to Caesarea was Nil's objective for today, and there in the city he could get help from the head of the Roman administration and garrison.

* * *

When they arrived in Caesarea and Nil left, the servant asked Temah:

"Don't ever make me pretend to be your servant again, Temah! And explain why you did not let us kill him?"

"Because, stupid, Roman officers don't travel alone," Temah said. "He was clearly on a mission, and if he disappeared, your whole village could be wiped out. How many times have I told you and your imbeciles not to attack Romans on your own? Even when you think that they are spies, like with this one. They endangered us all. Thanks Almighty, you brought him to me!"

"But you heard him, he was not on the mission," the man said. "At least, he was not really spying on us, like the people thought. He does not care about zealots; he was after Christians."

"And that's the reason why he should go unharmed," Temah said patiently. "He is after Christians, not us. Do you like Christians, Shaul?"

"Those dirty dogs? Traitors to our faith?" the man asked. "How could you even think that about me, Temah?"

"I don't," Temah said. "Just as long as this stupid Roman is against Christians, he does a good thing for us. So I wanted him to go free on his mission."

"I think that you let him go because you like Romans," Shaul said. "You are rich, and you trade with them. That's the reason you don't hate them as we do and as any true Jew must."

"Tsk-tsk-tsk, rich, poor, why do you think this matters, Shaul?" Temah asked. "You see, being a zealot is not about being rich or poor, it's about being a Jew. We are all Jews, true faithful Jews. And about my 'love' to Rome, did you hear what he said?"

"What?"

"On the third day of September Ides Rome is going to burn, and they will blame the Christians for that," Temah said. "You see, Shaul, I hate Rome. We all should hate Rome. Albinus is robbing us but he is the Roman procurator. He is sent to us from Rome. I'd love to see Rome burn."

"And what's here for us?" Shaul asked. "They are likely to raise taxes again to rebuild their precious capital, that's all."

"No, Shaul," Temah said. "It's not just our chance to strike back at the heart of the empire that oppresses us, it's our chance to take care of those pesky traitors, the Christians, as well. And don't forget, who missed those pests and let them go at large? Albinus! It's likely that he will be replaced then."

"Taking care of Christians?" Shaul asked. "Sounds good but what if Rome does not burn?"

"Oh, you look at the wrong side. What matters is that this stupid Roman will make sure that the Christians are blamed for it. That's why he had to go free."

"Temah, but what if it does not burn?" Shaul repeated.

"You see, if we are faithful enough, it will," Temah said and raised a finger. "That's our part, Shaul, to make sure it will."

THOSE SLY BASTARDS
Chapter IX, where we learn how disaster may be a source of hefty profits

Rome, Palatine Hill, palace, morning, hangover. The emperor opened his eyes and tried to focus them. The attempt failed miserably and brought back an attack of pain behind the eyes and in the temples. He stretched his hand and somebody put a cup into it. The emperor took a careful gulp, oh, good.... The servants knew well, Hyperborean drink went down, moisturizing the burning throat and stomach with an invigorating liquid. Now he was able to yawn, and scanty tears moistened the eyes. The sight improved, but still was not completely there. Maybe I should have some wine against a hangover instead of this salty drink, the thought came to his head. The thought of wine brought an attack of nausea. When it was over, the thought was not there anymore. Maybe it did not want to wait for so long, the emperor thought. Anyway, now he felt better.

He focused his eyes. Hall, the same hall with drunk guests, gloomy morning light, and doors to the garden. And Tigellinus, already dressed up in his full uniform, sitting in a chair and drinking something from a goblet. Maybe wine, subconsciousness obligingly suggested. Oh, no...

"Ophonius," the emperor called.

"Yes, Caesar?" Tigellinus said without getting up. He knew better than to tower over the recumbent emperor at this moment.

"Ophonius," the emperor said again. "This palace gives me nausea. I want a new one!"

"Whatever you wish, Caesar," Tigellinus said. "Just a different one?"

"No," the emperor said. "I want a completely new one, large, the whole area of Rome covered with just one huge palace." He stretched his hand, showing the size of the area. "Internal yards of the size of parks. I want to hunt in my backyard if I want to. And a lot of gold and gems, everywhere. I'll call it *Domus Aurea* – a Golden Palace, how do you like it? It should have whatever the best architects of Rome may imagine, so that I never get bored with it. How should we do that?"

"Well," Tigellinus said. "There may be a problem. It would take a lot of space, and there is not much vacant space in Rome. You know, the place where the Romans live."

"Why should I care about the Romans?" the emperor asked and sniffed. "Do they care about me? And why is it called 'Rome', I ask? Shouldn't it carry my name instead...?"

"As you wish, Caesar," Tigellinus said. "Anyway, first we need to clear up the space for such a palace. We need to clear it up from Romans as well as from the crummy hovels they live in. And then you need money."

"Money, always money," the emperor growled. "What are the provinces for?"

"Such a palace may need more than the provinces give us now," Tigellinus said.

"Then they should give us more," the emperor said. "Ophonius, help me out, I need fresh air."

Tigellinus helped him get up and they went out to the garden. The early beams of sun were slipping through the foliage of vines hiding the sky and lazily stirring under the cool morning breeze. The emperor sat on a stone bench and made a sign to Tigellinus to sit nearby.

"Speaking of money," he said, yawning, "do you think North Africa can pay more?"

"How do I know, Caesar?" Tigellinus said. "Macer is an able administrator, but if you question him, you need somebody who ruled there before, some former proconcul or procurator, at least."

"And who, do you think, this could be?" the emperor asked.

"Old Galba did a great job there about twenty years ago," Tigellinus said after a thought.

"Galba?" the emperor asked.

"Yes, the old Servius Galba. Claudius had problems in North Africa and he sent Galba there out of turn without drawing a lot. He ruled for just two years there, but he got everything in order, put Berberians in control, made shipments stable – he should know. He is also not interested in politics since that time. He is a priest in three colleges, but rather than that, he pays no attention to public affairs. So he is not likely to try to help Macer in any way. And he knows how to make money there. When he leaves the house, his slaves carry a million sesterces with him in a separate palanquin as spare change. He will be able to give good advice."

"See that he is invited tonight," the emperor said.

* * *

In the evening Galba came dressed in his white with purple stripes senatorial toga. He was a stout old man in his early sixties with short coarse gray hair. He wore no jewelry and sat, rigid and silent, among the crowd of motley-dressed everyday guests of the emperor trying to surpass each other in high-life talk and praises to the host. Galba paid respect to the food and the wine, but without any pretense and with such a stern look that people around him looked like a crowd of puffed up nobodies. Clearly that could not pass unnoticed.

"Are you going to praise the emperor, Galba, or did you just come to eat and drink?" one of the guests asked.

"No poem can grasp the greatness of Caesar, so any poem would be an abuse of his glory," Galba said. "And I am not a poet, I am a soldier. I'd rather honor the emperor with my silence, until he tells me to speak."

Everyone went silent looking at the emperor and expecting a fit of anger from him. Then Petronius, whom the emperor called *Arbiter Elegantiae* and whom he respected for his taste in fine arts, laughed up loudly.

"Well said, Galba. But I doubt that you are not a poet, as not many poets put their praises to Caesar so well."

The emperor listened to Petronius and then his face softened, he gave an approving smile, and everybody relaxed.

"Well said, old soldier," the emperor repeated Petronius' words. "As of telling you to speak, I need you to speak now and about things more important than praise. Follow me." The emperor stood up and went to the door. "Ophonius, you too."

Three men left the hall and the feast continued. The emperor left the palace and stood on the terrace near the entrance. Then he turned to Galba and Tigellinus who followed him.

"You were the proconcul of North Africa," he said. "I need your advice now."

"What do you want to know, Caesar?" Galba asked.

"You were told how much grain, oil, and money North Africa gave to Rome last year?" the emperor asked.

Galba nodded.

"Do you think that's a reasonable amount for this province? Can they give more?"

"Maybe," Galba said, then paused. "I've heard they have troubles with Berbers again, and there could be some excesses in place. From my experience I can say they can give probably ten to twelve percent more at most."

"Just that?" the emperor asked. "I hoped that they can give much more. Can they?"

"Forgive me, Caesar," Galba said, "but are you asking about grain, oil, or money? They are different things."

"Tell me about each of them."

"They cannot increase wheat production this year. Whatever they sowed is what they will get. But you can order them to sow more next year, so this can be improved fast. With oil, it takes years to grow a tree, so even if you order them to produce more, it will take time until they can give more oil. And about money, that depends on oil and wheat prices."

"How? I don't understand, you said these are different."

"Different indeed, Caesar. All the money they can give you comes from their sales of grain and oil. These are the only things this province really produces. The higher the prices, the more they get, and the more they get, the more they can pay you. But the more grain and oil they sell, the lower are the prices. You see, more oil and you lose in price, less oil and you lose in volume."

"Can you get more oil and more prices at the same time?" the emperor asked.

"Oh, no," Galba said. "You need a major disaster for that, and disasters are not good for the production."

"What kind of disaster?" Tigellinus asked.

"War, revolt, piracy, or something here, in Rome," Galba said. "It does not matter. Any disaster makes people worry and makes them ready to pay a higher price."

"Disaster!" The emperor sniffed then turned to Tigellinus, "Ophonius, are you talking about those Christians again?"

"Christians?" Galba asked.

"Yes," Tigellinus said. "Those bastards will try to burn Rome this autumn. Just keep it quiet, we are on it and will not let it happen. I don't want rumors."

"Don't worry," Galba said. "As you've seen, I am tacit on words. But it may be unfortunate if you prevent it."

"Why?" the emperor and Tigellinus asked almost together.

"I assume this palace costs a lot of money," Galba said. "With what you can get from North Africa and other provinces after such a fire, you can build twenty such palaces."

"How?" the emperor asked.

"You see, that's exactly what you asked before – high volume and high prices," Galba said. "A fire in Rome does not affect North Africa or transportation at all. Everything they grow and produce, they are still going to grow and produce. But the prices in Rome will go up. Here is the profit."

"No," Tigellinus said. "After such a fire we may have to decrease the prices or we will get a revolt on our hands."

"Of course," Galba agreed. "Every business requires initial expenses. You will decrease the prices at first to get the crowd happy, and then in a few months you'll let it soar higher than ever before. That's when you harvest your profit."

"That makes sense," the emperor said. "So how exactly will we profit from it? Wouldn't the olive tree growers get all the money?"

"No, Caesar, they will get nothing or almost nothing," Galba said. "They will still grow the same amount of olives, produce the same amount of oil, and still sell it all like nothing happened. Maybe they'll get a somewhat better price for it, but not by much. You see, the fire will happen in Rome, not in North Africa. North Africa will not be affected, so the price in North Africa will not rise much. The price will rise in Rome."

"So you say, the traders will profit?"

"For what they will buy there and sell here, yes," Galba agreed. "But because of the disaster in Rome, you can order the provincial governor to take control of the shipments. Then traders will just get mere transport expenses, which are still fixed and unaffected. Then all the profit is yours."

"How much are we talking about here?"

"Rome consumes annually roughly 100 million sextarius of olive oil at about two sesterces per sextarius, keeping in mind that some of it gets sour and sells cheaper," Galba said. "Raise the retail price for one sestercius, and you get a million golden aureii."

"You count better than a trader, soldier," the emperor said with a chuckle. "But not all oil comes from North Africa. Can you make the same with the oil coming from Greece, Spain, or Asia Minor?"

"That does not matter, Caesar," Galba said. "That's the beauty of the whole scheme. The only thing you need from North Africa is oil, not profits. The same with other provinces. The profit you make here in Rome, not there."

"And what about grain?"

"That may not be so easy," Galba said. "Egypt is a too strong and stable supplier of grain to shake the prices much with the events in Rome. It provides for one third of Roman grain, it's just too much. You need something to happen closer to Egypt to take advantage of that."

"What?"

"That I don't know, Caesar," Galba said. "Maybe some war or revolt? Not in Egypt itself, you don't want to compromise the source of grain, but somewhere nearby."

"Then oil," the emperor said after a pause. "Galba, I want you to supervise that I will get this million aureii."

"Forgive me, Caesar, I am old..." Galba started.

"You will have a province of your choice afterward," the emperor interrupted him. "Except North Africa, of course. We will need Macer's help as well."

"I always liked Hispania Tarraconensis," Galba said.

"You will get it."

"I'll take care of that for you, Caesar," Galba said and pressed his fist against his chest in a soft version of a legionnaire gesture. "Provided that Rome will burn in the autumn."

"Yes, provided that it will happen," the emperor said. "And we still want to prevent it. We are merely preparing the plans in case of a disaster, but we still want to prevent it. Ophonius, you've heard me!"

"Yes, Caesar!" Tigellinus nodded. "I've heard all."

"Good," the emperor said, turned around, and went back into the palace.

Two men were left alone on a quiet dark terrace. They looked at each other.

"Do you think you will be able to prevent this from happening, prefect?" Galba asked and look straight into the eyes of Tigellinus.

"I'll certainly do my best. You've heard the emperor," Tigellinus said returning a look.

"Good, good," Galba said and nodded in agreement. "We should defend Rome from those treacherous sly scoundrels. Be careful and thorough, Christians have a bad reputation, sly, cunning."

"My men are skillful, soldier," Tigellinus said with a light wry smile. "I've trained them well."

"Tithe," Galba said.

"Ten percent?" Tigellinus asked and smiled widely. "Thank you for the warning, Galba. I agree, those Christians are truly cunning and treacherous. Those sly bastards!"

LOVE THY NEIGHBOR
Chapter X, where we learn some exotic reasons for love

It was late when Nil arrived in Caesarea accompanied by the Good Samaritan and his "servant". On the way, Nil found that the procurator, Albinus, was in this city, not Jerusalem, so he decided to visit him tomorrow, first thing in the morning. With the document from Tigellinus, he was sure that he would be welcome enough to discuss the business. As of today, he found the local garrison, presented his credentials, ate a light supper, and went to sleep in the guest quarters. Staying at the garrison also took care of informing the procurator of his arrival, as the officer on duty immediately sent a soldier with the message.

Nil woke up early the next morning. While he looked for something to snack on, a soldier found him and informed him that the procurator expected him at his residence two hours after daybreak. Nil asked for directions and made his way to the rendezvous.

The city was mostly populated by Greeks and Jews, who left their heavy mark on it. Nil knew that there was a conflict between the city's Greek and Jewish communities and this was noticeable in the people's attitudes toward each other. Nil, in his obviously Roman attire, was catching sometimes aggressive, sometimes fearful looks from both sides. There was little surprise in that. As Nil was told, both communities believed that Romans allowed this conflict on purpose, and though nobody yet appealed to the Roman procurator, both parties believed the Romans favored their opponents.

Caesarea was architecturally built as a Roman city. However, despite the temples and palaces built in a Roman style, the city did not feel Roman. The people on the street were dressed oriental and behaved differently than in any Italian city. Poorer houses were built in a local style, and often had just a sheepskin in the doorway instead of an actual door. Eastern winds carried ochre dust from the mainland and hills year after the year. The streets and buildings were covered lightly with this dust, as if the city was a dark-skinned coquette who decided to cover her face with some lighter color. Or maybe an albino one who attempted to make her bluish face more vivid with an ochre powder. Both ways, she failed. The dust made the city look old and worn out.

Nil came closer to the harbor and the morning breeze brought the stink of foul water. The artificial harbor of Caesarea provided excellent protection against the waves of the open sea, but the circulation of water inside was not sufficient to wash away the garbage and rotting goods that spilled from the loading and unloading ships. That was especially true after the winter, when a number of ships were docked inside for months, waiting for *mare clausum* – the storm season – to end. Fortunately, Nil's road turned to the south, leaving the harbor on the right side. Nil passed a magnificent Temple of Caesar erected by the founder of the city, Herod the Great. Its white colonnade and red roof were the first things that seafarers saw when entering the harbor. Caesarea's style was not really Roman inside, but its façade was carefully designed to give this impression.

Nil passed on the right a huge pier with granaries and warehouses on it. The pier separated the harbor from the rest of the bay, so the air became fresh, only occasionally tainted with the smell of seaweed and rotten fish from the fishing boats that were not admitted into the harbor. Naturally, neither the king of Judea, nor Roman procurators wanted to breathe the port's miasmatic air, thought Nil.

He passed a large amphitheater on the left, and turned to the small peninsula, almost a cape, going well into the sea. It only had enough space for just one palace – the Palace of Herod the Great. That was the residence of the Roman procurators of *Provincia Iudaea* for decades.

The palace had a garden shadowed with olive and cypress trees in front of it. It was separated from the mainland by a stone wall of local ochre sandstone. With the other three sides going right into the water, the palace had a good defensive position as well as evacuation routes, just in case. The palace was done in Roman style, with white columns, portico, open indoor yard with a pool surrounded by a colonnade visible from outside, and red, almost flat roofs on top of individual structures. An alley, paved with shaggy stone slabs of local white limestone, led from the gates to the main entrance. The Roman guards at the gates expected Nil and let him in as soon as he presented himself. And so did the guards at the entrance.

Albinus met Nil on the paved patio facing the open sea. A low parapet on paunchy round pillars, made of some white stone, separated the patio from the precipice going into the sea. The light morning breeze made the air humid and salty, and the view of the sea sparkling under the morning sun was a magnificent match to the architecture of the palace.

"When I am here, I forget that I rule this crippled piece of land which is called a province out of misunderstanding," Albinus said. He was a lean strong man in his middle fifties with marks of gray on his head. He was dressed in a white tunic and a toga, as appropriate for his rank, but Nil noticed that he was just as accustomed to armor, a military lacerna cloak, and a helmet with the red comb. He wore no jewelry except his gold equestrian ring, but, again, Nil knew that ruling this province made him a rich man. Of course, this was not North Africa or Egypt, but still, the post of procurator gave a lot of opportunities to improve one's finances, including tax collection and mere bribes. He probably got this position through relations with the old patrician family of Albinus, Nil decided.

"No significant resources, land is mostly a desert, no significant production of anything except dust, and prophets by the dozen," Albinus continued. "And the people are a bunch of shepherds struggling to sustain themselves and revolting occasionally out of despair. A truly pathetic estate of Rome. We are only here to prevent Parthians from establishing a presence en route of shipments of Egyptian grain to Rome. Anyway, the courier said that you have a message from Tigellinus. What have you brought to me?"

"Trouble, I'm afraid, procurator," Nil answered. "We have reliable information that the Jewish sect called Christians is going to try to burn Rome on the third day of September Ides. I am sent to investigate their roots in Judea and Egypt, as it seems that they will employ help there."

"Trouble, indeed," Albinus smiled. "How reliable are the sources? Those Christians, they are disgusting, no doubt, but to burn Rome? Actually, in case of a revolt, they are that rare kind of Jews that I don't expect much trouble from."

"Very reliable, procurator," Nil said. "And from several independent sources. However, we suspect more Egyptian Christians and their connection to Egyptian priests rather than the ones from Judea. Anyway, because the whole sect came from Judea, it's prudent to check here as well. Can I ask if you have any information that may indicate possible trouble from them?"

"No," Albinus said after a short consideration. "Nothing. As I said, the Christians may be a little annoyance but that's all. It could be some new sect of them that you are talking about. But thanks for the warning. I will keep an eye on them and inform Rome if I discover anything worth attention. Anything else?"

"We know the name of their leader," Nil said. "He's called Benjamin, and he is probably a trader who deals with Greeks a lot. He is likely from Judea or Crete. Hope this will help your investigation here. That's it, procurator. With your permission, I'll leave for Egypt tomorrow. That's where my main investigation is going to be."

"Good," Albinus said. He started to raise his hand to give a dismissive gesture, but stopped. "You know, I am going to Jerusalem in a few days. There I will meet with the High Priest. He is loyal to us, just out of fear, of course, but it may be worth talking to him about those Christians. He may know something. Stay here in Caesarea and accompany me to Jerusalem."

"Yes, procurator," Nil said. "One more thing… I need some money. I was robbed on the way to Caesarea."

"Robbed?" Albinus frowned. "Who dared to rob a Roman citizen and an official in my province?"

"I don't know," Nil said. "Some dirty and poor crowd on the road about a dozen miles to the north of Caesarea, right on the shore."

"I'll have to look at this matter too," Albinus said and clapped his hands. A guard came from inside the house. "Take my guest to the paymaster and tell him to pay travel and living expenses for a month to this man from the imperial business fund."

"Thank you, procurator," Nil said.

"Don't mention it," Albinus answered. "Now about Jerusalem – I am going there in two days, on the thirteenth day of May Calends. Be here at the palace the same time as today. You will stay at the garrison, right?"

Nil nodded.

"See you in two days," Albinus said, and turned back to him.

The guard showed the way to the paymaster, and Nil got his money. He did not feel bad for reporting being robbed, after all he was attacked. This was not even theft; everybody did it if they could. Just one more perk in the service of the emperor.

* * *

Procurators usually don't travel light, and Albinus was not an exception. He was accompanied by a few officials of his administration, Nil, and two cohorts with an auxiliary *ala* of Syrian horsemen. Cohorts and ala were supposed to take care of the palace security during his stay, as well as any other unexpected needs that the procurator may have in the capital of a troubled province. Nil got a horse, as well as officials. The old bureaucrats are not quite comfortable on the horseback, Nil thought with a smile, watching how a fat scribbler was trying to get into the saddle on a strong bay horse. Albinus could have a chariot, but he preferred to ride a stout black stallion. He dressed in light armor and sat firmly and comfortably in the horned military saddle like he was born to it.

The distance to Jerusalem could be covered in two days on a forced march, but Albinus did not want to enter the city in the dark. He'd rather come in the day, when more people could see him and the marching soldiers as a reminder of imperial power. So they stayed the first night in a field, and the second night near a small city less than ten miles from Jerusalem.

After they reached the city at last and the initial ceremonies were done, Albinus let Nil know that the conversation would take place tomorrow, and retreated with the King of Judea, Agrippa the Second, into some back rooms of the palace to discuss current affairs. So Nil, accompanied by Furius, the *princeps prior* and the third centurion of the second cohort, with whom he made friends during his few days in Caesarea, left the palace and went to the city looking for the little joys of a military soul – the places with wine and girls.

The place was found easily shortly after they left the palace complex. Not that it would be easy alone, as unpaved streets, or rather earth roads, going up and down, were filled with almost identical buildings that carried no hints of such places. And having everything tinted in different shades of dusty gray and ochre did not help either. Maybe Jews had the places to drink and enjoy themselves, but it was almost impossible to recognize a difference between stores, workshops, and dwelling places, which were sometimes elaborate in a distinctive eastern style and sometimes as simple as a hole in the wall or the side of a hill. To give the city credit, Nil noticed, following his friend, that the dirt was honest dirt, no slops and human excrement like in some other cities. Jerusalem already had the sewer and after Romans established their control of the city, they built aqueducts to provide inhabitants with fresh water.

Fortunately, Furius was here before and he led Nil to a Roman-style place that specialized in serving the local garrison and visitors to the city. The place did not differ much from the outside. It was a two-story building made of the same yellowish gray stone as many other buildings around. Only a picture of an amphora and a goblet, drawn on the wall above the wooden door, indicated the purpose of the place. They sat at the empty corner of a long table. There were a few other visitors in the tavern who sat in small groups of two to five men and had a quiet talk. The owner, a fidgety and elderly Greek who somehow managed to do business in this city, brought wine and some food, and after the second pitcher, Nil found himself talking again about his mission. Actually, he already told Furius everything he could back in Caesarea, but as the conversation mostly consisted of bashing the Christians, and Furius did not favor them either, it was pretty much small talk to accompany drinking.

"Excuse me." A tall bearded man approached them. He was dressed in a multicolored robe, with a piece of white fabric covering his head, red leather boots, and a blade on a rich, wide, embroidered belt. His Latin was not perfect, but fairly decent for an oriental man, decent enough to suspect a good private education. "I've accidentally overheard your conversation, and it seems like you are not simply bashing those Christians, but looking for something about them. I assume, you are not mere legionaries?"

"You bet," Furius said with a laugh. "I am a centurion, and this guy is on a special mission from Rome to investigate those bastards!"

"I think I could be of an assistance." The man gave a soft smile and a light bow that looked more like a relaxed nod of approval. He turned to Nil. "May I know how I can address you? You see, my king is very concerned about this sect, and because of my job I have to keep an eye on them. So I may know something of importance for you."

"My name is Nil Septimus," said Nil. "And who the hell are you?"

"Nil." The man smiled again, ignoring apparent rudeness. "Then call me Maalish. I am in the service of the King Malchus. So may I know, what concerns do you have about those Christians, so that I can see if I know anything of relevance to you?"

"Why the hell not," Nil said. The local wine clearly did not work well for him, as usually he was more polite. "Did you hear anything about the Christians planning to make big trouble somewhere?"

"They don't have to, Nil Septimus, they are trouble by themselves," Maalish said. "Can you be more specific?"

"I mean real trouble, like trying to burn a whole city," Nil said. "Maybe even Rome."

"Christians trying to burn Rome," Maalish said, visibly amused by the idea. "I have to admit, I've never heard something like that, although now that you mention it, it makes sense. These dogs hate Rome. I'll alert the spies of my king to look for that. Whom should we inform if we find something about that?"

"Rome," Nil said. "Inform the prefect of Praetorian Guards, Ophonius Tigellinus."

"That high," Maalish said. "Then it looks like it's serious. Should I know anything else?"

"No," Nil said. "How do I know who you are?"

"I understand." Maalish gave again his semi-bow, turned away, and left the tavern.

"Who do you think he is?" Nil asked.

"How do I know?" Furius answered. "I'd say he was asking too many questions to be an accidental man."

"Are you acquainted with the Great Vizier?" the publican asked, appearing near the table.

"Great Vizier?" Nil asked.

"Yes, he is the Great Vizier of the Kingdom of Arabia," the publican said. "He accompanies their prince Rabbel. He is visiting King Agrippa on some state business. I thought this is why the procurator came here, to talk to both of them."

"You seem to be very well informed. How do you know Maalish?" Nil said.

" 'Maalish'?" The publican laughed shortly. "That's not his name. 'Maalish' means 'Never mind' in their language. And about being informed, one has to be if he wants to have business around. You know, this place is not very friendly to foreigners. You should keep your eyes open."

Nil and Furius returned late from the city and Nil immediately went to bed. In the morning he was woken up by a soldier.

"The procurator wants you to talk to the Great Vizier of Arabia," a legionnaire said. "I'll show you the way. They are already waiting."

Nil got up, dressed, and followed the soldier. Maalish, or whatever his name was, met him in one of the rooms in another wing of the palace. He was accompanied by another man who was young but dressed in the same style and also bright and rich.

"Now, I believe, you know who I am," said vizier, "and I'll be glad to be of assistance to the empire. This is my trusted man; you can talk to him as it was me. Now, can you give me more details at what to look for?"

"Sure," Nil said. "Why did you give such a name to me?"

"I have to apologize for that," vizier smiled. "I never thought that Romans have a name 'Nil', it means 'nothing' in your language, right? And Nothing the Seventh looked like a pseudonym. So I just decided to return the courtesy and gave a pseudonym myself. So, about the business?"

"We know for sure that Christians, or maybe some internal sect of theirs, will try to burn Rome," Nil said. "Make your men look for any hints about that. We also know the name of their leader. It's some trader called Benjamin from Crete or Judea. If

71

you learn anything about him or the plan, inform Rome. Myself, if possible, or you know whom. That's it."

"Yes, I know," vizier nodded. "For how long should we look for them?"

"If nothing happens on the third day of September Ides, don't bother anymore," Nil said and shrugged his shoulders. "That will mean that we took care of them."

"Anything else?"

"No, that's pretty much all we know for now," Nil said.

Vizier gave a dismissive gesture and Nil left.

After his steps fell silent, the man turned to vizier.

"So, what do you think?"

"First, we will look for this Benjamin and keep an eye on Christians, of course," vizier said respectfully. "Just like we promised this Roman."

"I like this 'first'." The man smiled. "You're clearly thinking in the right direction. Go on."

"I think," vizier said, "that if this man fails to prevent the fire, the Romans will be busy punishing Christians."

"They will be busy punishing Judea," the man corrected him.

"Why, my prince?"

"The Roman barbarians don't see the difference between Christians and Jews. In the actual city they may prosecute Christians selectively, but it's likely that they would want a piece of Judea as well. And then…" Prince Rabbel paused.

"Then they will be too busy to try to annex Arabia," vizier concluded with a smile.

"That does not mean that we don't like Romans," the prince said. "We will even help them with Judea by giving auxiliaries. Say, a thousand of our horsemen."

Vizier smiled in return.

"I see why my father entrusted you with your post," the prince said with a smile. "You know, those Christians say 'love thy neighbor', and I would really love them and Jews for keeping Romans off our backs."

Vizier smiled and bowed slightly.

"And you know, I would really love the man—" the prince stopped smiling and looked into vizier's eyes, "—who will make sure that Jews and Christians keep Romans off our backs."

"I am sure your benevolence will not be wasted, my prince," vizier said with a smile, clasping his hands to his heart and giving a bow.

I'LL SEND THE PEOPLE
Chapter XI, where, for a change, we meet two people who don't want Rome to burn

The conversation with Nabatheans – that's what the people of the Kingdom of Arabia were called – left Nil baffled at why they were so insistent in helping with the case. Granted, Nil thought, all these small kings, in almost client status to the empire, were trying to keep the favor of Rome, but this was clearly a far stretch from normal. They could grovel out of fear but going as far as asking the procurator for information? Even the province authorities would not press for accepting their help after the investigator from metropolis suggested they go to hell. And that was pretty much what Nil said to the vizier yesterday in the tavern. So how is it that representatives of a formally independent king, who was usually somewhat jealous in internal affairs, still pushed to be involved? Nil heard how, about three decades ago, before Caligula seized Damascus from Arabia, Roman agents had to hide from the city guards during their missions. Aretas IV, who was king of Arabia at the time, did not fancy agents of the empire working in his territory. Something does not add up, Nil decided, but hey, no harm done. If they help, so much the better, if not, who cares? Anyway, it was the procurator's order to tell them, he concluded the thought with satisfaction.

Today he was ordered to stay in the palace and wait until he was invited to the conversation. Albinus had a number of issues to discuss with Jerusalem authorities and Nil's topic was just one of them. On the other hand, as a person close to the procurator and a guest in the palace, Nil was accommodated with all the comfort possible, so he did not have much to complain about, other than being bored with waiting. And even the boredom was tamed by food, wine, and an Egyptian slave girl. Being raised in Rome, King Herod Agrippa II knew how to please his guests, although being conscious of local habits and sensitivity, he preferred not to offer Jewish slaves to serve foreigners.

If he had them at all, Nil thought. The province was poor for a reason. Harsh natural conditions made slavery inefficient. When a man can produce barely enough to feed himself, you don't benefit much from making him work for you. As a result, few in Judea, whether Greek or Jew, owned slaves, and if they did, practiced patriarchal-style slavery in which the slaves were essentially part of the family. The only exception was with rich people and state owned slaves. Well, Nil thought, it's not that different from Rome after all. The only difference is that there is way more rich people in Rome.

The whole day passed before Nil was asked to join the procurator in a large hall. The doors in the back were open to a gallery facing west, and hall was slowly darkening with the sun setting down. Albinus was talking to three other men, apparently representatives of the local power. All four were standing some distance from the doors to the gallery, but close enough to benefit from the fresh air coming into the hall from there.

Nil had already seen the king. Agrippa was dressed in a Roman tunic and toga. Being raised at the imperial court, he probably looked Roman even more than Albinus. Not so were the two other men. One was an elderly man in his early sixties with a gray beard and a moustache and a strict, stately, and significant expression on his face. He wore a sleeveless pullover made of a thick wool on top of a blue linen tunic that was going down to the floor. Multicolored threads of the pullover blended together into a dark lilac, somewhat brownish color. A golden plate with different colored gems was fixed to his chest by a yellow belt. This was accompanied by a dark blue turban-like hat on his head.

Another man was dressed similarly, except that his pullover was plain dark blue and he did not wear the golden plate. Anyway, their clothes looked almost black in the fading light of the setting sun. It strikingly contrasted with the white Roman togas of the king and the procurator. The second man was in his earlier thirties. His beard was not touched by gray and his face was respectful and expecting. Although, if somebody asked Nil which of the two he would rather see as an enemy, he would not be quite sure what to answer. With his trained eye, Nil could see a dangerous and powerful man behind the meek and subservient façade. The Governor of the Temple had very much the same functions as the first priest in some Egyptian temples. He was the head of the internal police of the Temple and sometimes carried more actual power than the formal head.

"Here is Nil Septimus, the man from Rome I told you about," Albinus said when Nil entered the hall. "Nil, Caesar Agrippa—" the procurator gave a nod in the direction of the king, who was given the honorary title of Caesar of Judea by the Roman Senate "—wants to help investigate your case. These are the High Priest Ananias and the Governor of the Temple Eleazar. They have the people to carry out a local investigation. Describe the case."

"We have reliable data that the Christians, or some new sect within the Christians, are going to try to burn Rome on the third day of September Ides," Nil said. "We know the name of his leader. It's some trader named Benjamin, probably, from Judea or Crete. He deals a lot with Greeks and is involved in selling goods in Rome. We know that he is trading oil for sure. We suspect that he will employ support from Egypt and, maybe, Egyptian priests, but he may also have local support here in Judea, because that's where the Christians came from. That's pretty much all we know for now."

"Not very much," Eleazar, the younger of the priests, said thoughtfully. "Although, I'd like to meet this Benjamin of yours."

"Me too," said Ananias, the older priest with his eyes now betraying a cruel old man behind the stately mask.

"Me too," the king said. "And I am deadly serious about that. I expect you two to put your best people at work to give me and the procurator such an opportunity."

"Also, we are wondering if you already know anything that can help with the investigation?" the procurator asked. "We know you keep an eye on those Christians, so I guess some information may have crossed your path before."

The king looked at Eleazar.

"Unfortunately, no, nothing like that," the young priest said. "But we will keep our eyes open. Frankly, I am not surprised. That's the sort of thing you would expect from those traitors of our faith. As to Benjamin, this is a very popular name in Judea. I am sure we've heard about a lot of Christians called Benjamin. The question is if we have heard about that particular Benjamin."

"Thank you," Albinus said. "I hope you will be able to find the guy and prevent the disaster."

"I think we all know what you hope for," Ananias said with narrowed, angry eyes. "You'd like this to happen. Christians, Jews – who cares? As long as you can destroy us and cover your deeds."

"Ananias!" Agrippa said.

"No, let him continue," Albinus answered coldly. "What deeds, High Priest?"

"Taxation that exhausted the country. Bribes to let the criminals out of prisons. Robbers that you cover up as long as they share with you," Ananias said. "Oh, you would love to have a new war on us, to destroy us and keep all these crimes of yours hidden. Don't worry, procurator. We'll find these criminals, if they ever existed. We know what is at stake."

"I'll talk to you later," Albinus said to Nil and gave a dismissive gesture. After Nil left, he said, "And now it seems all for today. I'd rather retire for now. Let's continue tomorrow."

"See you tomorrow, Albinus," Agrippa said with a nod, and the procurator left the hall. Three men were standing in the darkening hall. Then the king said, "I'll retire for today too. You can go. See that what we discussed today is taken care of. I especially want you to be on the lookout for this Benjamin and Christians. I don't want the wrath of Rome on my people, and you may be right, Ananias – I am not sure they will differentiate us from those traitors."

"Yes," the High Priest said. "Eleazar will put his best men on the case."

When Agrippa left, the priests were left alone.

"Do you really want me to find and arrest this Benjamin, father?" Eleazar asked. "For a change, Christians are going to do a very good thing. They will teach Roman barbarians a lesson and bite them back. We prayed in our Temple for three centuries before the ancestors of those barbarians raped Sabine women to conceive the first Romans. And that's what they are doing with the rest of the world. Wouldn't it be wonderful, if somebody gave a little back? And afterward, with the wrath of Rome on

Christians, we could give away all those traitors to Romans. And enough wood to crucify them all, if they want. Wouldn't you like to bite Rome back and take care of those traitors in a single shot?"

"For a change," the High Priest frowned, "Agrippa said the right thing. You are too young, you don't understand. You are right in saying that the Romans are barbarians. They think that Christians are just one more Jewish sect, nothing more. This Roman is an expert, he knows the difference, but most Romans and Caesar don't. They will punish us for their sins. I want you to find this Benjamin and make sure nothing happens that may endanger us. We already quarreled with Babylon, and you know the result. The Temple was destroyed and we spent 70 years in captivity, until Cyrus came and allowed us to return to Jerusalem and rebuild the Temple. Don't quarrel with this second Babylon – Rome – and our people will be around to see the third, and the fourth one. Challenge it, and we may have to wait too long for the second Cyrus to return us home."

"Father, are you afraid of Rome?" Eleazar asked.

"Yes, I am afraid of Rome, son," Ananias said. "And you should be too. And stop these Pharisee's tricks. They managed to get the Roman eagle down from the gates of the Temple, but they will not help us when the Roman eagles come to us carried by the Roman legions. And make sure that those Christians do not try their stupid conspiracy. You have enough men to investigate and prevent that."

"As you wish father," Eleazar said and gave a soft bow. "I will go even so far as to send a few of my men to Rome. Just to make sure that Christians don't burn Rome." He paused, and then added with a respectful and significant smile, "That those Christians don't burn Rome on the third day of September Ides right after the sunset. Let's go, father, we've had a tough day."

Eleazar turned away and walked out of the hall. Ananias followed him with his eyes, sighed, shook his head contritely, and walked out of the hall after his son.

* * *

Soon after Nil returned to his room, a soldier came in with a message that Albinus wanted to see him again. Nil followed the messenger to a triclinium, which was a part of the procurator's accommodations in the palace. He was already there, reclined on a couch, alone in the room. It was dark and the light from a couple of torches was poor and fluctuating. There was no food on the table, just wine.

"Be my guest," Albinus said, pointing to another couch.

Nil thanked him with a nod and reclined in front of his host with a goblet of wine in his hand.

"How do you like this?" Albinus said. "Dirty dogs. Suspicious of each other and of everyone they come around. If not for us, they would fight each other to death unless taken over by Parthians or Nabatheans of Arabia, and still they hate us. Anyway, at least they will really be looking for your incendiaries."

"I hope so," Nil agreed.

"What I called you for," Albinus said, "is to tell you that I am sending a courier to Rome the day after tomorrow. You can send any correspondence you need with him. There is a trireme going to Ostia soon, so your messages will be in the hands of the prefect in a couple of weeks. You can send personal correspondence as well if you wish."

"Thank you, I'll certainly use this opportunity," Nil said. The old bureaucrat wants to know what I will report back to Tigellinus, he decided.

"And one more thing," Albinus said. "Don't mention those silly accusations you heard today, would you?"

"Of course," Nil said. And you are definitely afraid of those accusations, he thought, but why should I care? "I'll just write that locals are hostile and rebellious, and that you handle them capably and well."

"That would be quite correct," Albinus said with a nod. "I guess you will be leaving soon?"

"Yes," Nil said. "I am going to Egypt. There my main investigation will take place."

"I'll send you the paymaster with six months of travel and living expenses for your trip," Albinus said. "I would recommend to take a sea route; it's much faster. Meanwhile, feel free to stay at the palace with me for a few days to rest before continuing your journey."

"Thank you, procurator. I'll mention in my message how helpful you were in the investigation, as well as praise your administration of the province."

"You are welcome," Albinus said with a smile. "It's always a pleasure to talk to an intelligent person."

A PROVINCE, YOU WON'T MISS
Chapter XII, where we see what is the use of being the emperor's wife

What's the use of being a wife of the emperor, if your husband uses any opportunity to look at other women, Poppaea thought while relaxing in a bath tub filled with jennet milk. The mosaic decorated *tepidarium*, the warm room of the palace thermae, was equipped with this bath tub specially for this morning routine of the queen. Not exactly the queen, she thought, annoyed. Rome does not have a queen. I am just the wife of the emperor. Just another wife instead of a murdered Octavia.

Poppaea was a beautiful young woman in her mid-twenties. She already had a son from a previous marriage, and last year she had a girl, who survived barely long enough for the celebrations in her honor. After having two children, a woman has to worry about how she looks, especially if her husband can choose any woman he wants. And Poppaea did worry. The best stylists cared for her long dark hair, masseurs treated her well-proportioned body and muscles, and this milk bath was supposed to keep her skin white and tight. That's not to mention jewelry, cosmetics, and the best dress and footwear the empire could provide for the first lady.

The morning was irrecoverably spoiled. Usually, it was the time when Poppaea gained self-confidence and a strength for the day to come. She started to take these baths following the recipe of the legendary Egyptian Queen Cleopatra to keep her beauty from aging. Whether it helped or not, it was hard to say, but it definitely helped her feel self-confident in her powers over her husband. It usually felt like the mystic powers of the legendary queen flowed inside her, giving her an influence to start wars and destroy empires.

Today, it did not feel as good. Amusingly enough, the reason for that, not to mention the husband, was her old friend named Cleopatra. Named after the queen, she was the one who told Poppaea the ancient rejuvenating secret of the milk baths. Cleopatra was only a few years older than Poppaea. She was married to a relatively insignificant and short-tempered man of a not very good origin named Gessimus Florus. He also had a reputation of being greedy and grubby in his deals, but, well, so was Tigellinus, Poppaea thought with a sneer. Not much harm for the imperial family reputation anyway.

As ill luck would have it, the culprit of her sad thoughts, Cleopatra, entered the room. She often accompanied Poppaea in the morning so the servants let her in without any questions. In fact, occasionally Poppaea allowed her friend to use the milk bath after she finished with it. Maybe that's why my philanderer spent last evening looking at her, she thought.

"Salve, Poppaea. It's a good morning outside," Cleopatra said with a simple-minded, friendly expression on her face. She took off her *stola*, a long tunic worn by Roman matrons, and submerged into the warm water pool.

"Outside, maybe," Poppaea answered.

"Oh, dear, is anything wrong?" Cleopatra asked.

"You," Poppaea said, looking at her friend's white neck, graceful shoulders, and tight, full breasts. Yes, this may be a danger, she thought. She already was accustomed to her husband having occasional sex with any woman he chose to. However, it's one thing to have an occasional "hit and run"; having a woman who is accepted in the house and can build her influence over time is much more serious. "Yesterday my goat spent the whole evening staring at you."

"Oh, my!" Cleopatra tossed her hands against her mouth. "I thought it only looked so to me. Poppaea, you know, I'd never think of such things. What can I do?"

"Get out of his sight for a while," Poppaea said. Or I will get you out of his sight, she added mentally.

"Oh, my, I will," Cleopatra said. "You know, I am not fit for politics, I simply will not survive it. They will kill my husband, and then me, when the emperor gets bored with me. Poppaea, will you help me?"

"Help you?"

"Yes, you remember? You promised to ask the emperor if he could give my husband a good place somewhere," Cleopatra said. "Could he give Gessimus some province? Then my husband will have to leave Rome and I will follow him and we all will be safe."

"Yes, I remember," Poppaea said. She really wanted to ask for this favor, but she did not want to let Cleopatra go – she was such a good companion. But now, she thought, it may be a good time. I am not cruel by nature, not more cruel than many others, she noticed mentally while starting to relax in the bath. Besides, today Cleopatra, tomorrow it could be somebody less cooperative and more dangerous. Poppaea raised her arms from the bath and looked at her white, clean skin and elegant hands. I am still very attractive and I can hold him for quite a while, she thought, but it may be really nice to have a governor of some province owe me. Just in case I have to flee the city for my life. And to have a governor whose wife owes me is even better, she concluded.

"Will you?" Cleopatra asked.

"Yes, I will," Poppaea said. "I'll talk to him today if he is in the right mood."

"Oh, thank you! Thank you!" Cleopatra said. "What do you think I should do, meanwhile? Should I go to my villa outside the city?"

"No, don't. If you run, he will try to catch you," Poppaea said. "Just try to be more bland, put less ceruse on your face, make a simpler hairdo. He thinks he is a great artist, so he would not pursue an artless person out of fear of being considered artless himself. And for gods sake, show some affection to your own husband. Mine thinks that's so vulgar, he'll walk away from you like you have plague. And in case you have other ideas…" She looked at Cleopatra and paused.

"Oh, no, I will not," Cleopatra said. "I'll do everything you say. Just, please, try to get this place for Gessimus. You know," she waved her hands, "how long can I show affection for him?"

Poppaea and Cleopatra laughed in an instant. Gessimus was clearly not a dream husband for a Roman woman. He was not ugly, but almost as faded and dull as a man can be. His grubbiness in deals brought him a bad reputation, and that was not good for a career. The blunt and greedy martinet had one more serious defect that a man can have – he was neither rich nor influential.

"Did you see Grecina yesterday on the Forum," Poppaea asked. "The old hen made a hairdo like she was trying to seduce Jupiter himself."

"Yes, I saw her." Cleopatra waved her hands and laughed again. "People say their nephew came to live with them for a while. He is a nice boy, no doubt, but does she have to be so obvious?"

Poppaea relaxed. At last the bath started to work as it did before. She felt self-confident and in control now. Who cares that the emperors rule the empires? As long as their wives rule the emperors, she thought with a smile. I may even allow Cleopatra to use the jennet milk bath after myself today. She is a good gal, obedient and nice. She will have a good use for her young skin among the wild Gauls, the unrefined Thracians, or the fierce Nubians, Poppaea grinned mentally. Or wherever her husband is sent, as long as it is far from Rome.

* * *

The emperor rehearsed his singing for the evening. Today was the last day of *Vinalia*, the six day wine-drinking festival, and he decided to treat the guests tonight with his singing. It was the middle of the day. He ordered everybody out of the garden and tried to sing a new poem, he wrote yesterday, in complete seclusion. Or almost complete. Poppaea took an active part in driving everybody out of the garden, and that left her the only privileged and benevolent spectator of the rehearsal.

The poem was terrible. He blended together the pieces of poetic exercises of his guests, who were not quite sober when suggesting the pieces. Then he connected them with clumsy verses, making the whole thing look like a Babylonian tower devoted to everything and nothing in particular. The singing was not much better either. The emperor exerted himself, hissed, produced hoarse sounds, hit sour notes, but continued.

"Splendid! Beautiful!" Poppaea exclaimed after each verse and accompanied that by exalted applause with her miniature, fine-molded palms. "Maginificent!" She looked at him with her large, lustrous eyes so sincerely that nobody would have guessed that she did not actually listen. She applauded not the singer, but the emperor. Her Emperor. The man who ruled the world and put her on the top of it together with himself. Isn't it really splendid and magnificent? Occasionally she thought about how he would sing tonight, and how the people around him would have to praise and applaud his singing. Then she laughed so sincerely that the emperor felt like it was the highest praise an artist could get.

After a bit, he got tired and stopped.

"Beautiful! Excellent!" Poppaea applauded, with her eyes shining with joy. "You should definitely sing for the guests today. I don't know if they deserve that, but you're so generous."

The emperor, red and sweaty from the effort, sat in the chair near her.

"I'll dedicate this poem to you," he said, trying to breathe normally. "By the way, about the guests... is your friend invited? I think her name is Cleopatra, like the former Egyptian queen, right?"

"Yes." Poppaea put herself on guard. "I think she is. Speaking of her, could you give her husband, Gessimus Florus, a province for a couple of years?"

"Gessimus?" the emperor asked. "Why?"

"She is my friend. We talk a lot about each other's lives, share our little secrets. She is my very good friend," Poppaea said. She noticed with satisfaction how her husband's face pulled at the mention of her friendship and confidence in each other's affairs.

"I don't know," the emperor said. "If she goes with him, whom will you entrust your secrets?"

"You!" Poppaea said with a smile. "Of course, she will go with him. She loves him so much. She may be one of the most devoted matrons in whole Rome," Poppaea stressed 'matron' as if the speech was about some elderly housewife. "Besides, they are a perfect match to each other. She is so bland and artless, and he is blunt and rude. She is a good friend, but you know..." She smiled, letting her husband finish the sentence by himself. "Of course, you know, with your taste for elegance. She is artless, such a simpleton. Oh, don't tell me you are interested in her!"

"Sure," the emperor said. He noticed the jealous notes in his wife's voice, and he was not willing to admit an interest in an artless person either. "I'll talk to Ophonius to see if we have something around for him."

"My hero," Poppaea said, sat at his feet, embraced his legs, and put her head on his knees.

* * *

In the evening he sang the new poem. Applause and praises were loud and continued almost as long as the poem itself. Then the emperor left the room to drink warm milk with honey to soften his overworked throat. Tigellinus accompanied him as usual.

"Ophonius," the emperor said, coughing slightly to clear his throat. "Do you think they liked it?"

"Oh, for sure," Tigellinus said. "You've heard them praising you. Only I don't think they got why you dedicated it to Poppaea."

"That's my poem," the emperor said. "I can dedicate it to whoever I want to."

"Sure thing."

"Speaking of Poppaea, do you think we can give Gessimus Florus some province to rule for a couple of years?"

"Gessimus?" Tigellinus asked. "Why? He is grubby, thievish, and insignificant. Besides he is blunt and arrogant. He'll make any province revolt in two years. Not that this is much of a problem, but not a reason either."

"His wife is a good and confident friend of Poppaea. She asked me today," the emperor said. "Besides, I just want that. Who is Caesar here?"

"Both are quite good reasons," Tigellinus agreed without even a slight sign of mockery. "I foresee only one problem with that."

"What's the problem?"

"If you want to actually give something to Gessimus, you may need a province that you won't miss," Tigellinus said.

THAT REQUIRES SOME MONEY
Chapter XIII, where Nil gets help that many would not expect

Nil wrote the message the next day and handed it over to the courier. He had no doubts that Albinus would read it before letting it go to the destination. But, hey, he decided, six month's pay is a hefty sum and definitely worth some creative writing. So he spent some time praising the administrative abilities of the procurator and painting locals as rebellious scum that would have revolted long ago if they had not been under the capable Albinus' rule.

He spent a couple more days in Jerusalem, and after that left for the nearest sea port, Joppa. After considering his experience near Caesarea, Nil decided to equip himself with some light Greek-style leather armor and a *gladius* – the standard issue legionnaire sword. Local stores did not carry much Roman military stuff, but the cohorts had some spare inventory and after an evening in the city and a monetary gift, *pilus prior* – the centurion on command of the second cohort – who was also an old friend of Furius was persuaded to share some of this inventory with Nil. The favorable disposition of the procurator did not hurt either.

The way to Joppa was quite uneventful. Nobody considered Nil a spy on the road, neither did anybody attempt to confess to him about the sinister plans of the trader Benjamin. So after spending most of the day in the saddle, he arrived at the city. Nil left the horse at the local *mansio* – imperial post station – and headed to the port to find a ship to Alexandria.

Joppa had a long and stormy history. Being one of the oldest cities around, it changed hands many times, being Caanite, Egyptian, Phoenician, and Greek. Now, for almost two centuries, it was firmly Jewish, although as in any port, a lot of Greeks and many others were present as well. The city was built around a hill facing the sea, and the legend said that right at the foot of the hill was the rock where Andromeda was chained as sacrifice to the sea monster. The rock was there, all right, complete with the iron ring in it. As to the rest of the story... there was no proof that Perseus did not really rescue the Ethiopian princess here long ago, and that was good enough for the locals.

A rocky coast, open to the waves, made it complicated to dock, so most ships had to anchor about a mile away in the sea, and crews had to use small boats to come ashore or to move the merchandize. Still, the port was fairly well used as it was the closest port to Jerusalem – about a day's travel closer than Caesarea. It was also the end of one of the land routes from Arabia that brought exotic spices and fragrances to the sea shore.

Where do you find a ship if they are all anchored a mile away from the shore? In the tavern. Nil sat on a bench at the end of a long table, dropped a couple of small coins and requested a mug of wine and a handful of the last year pickled olives as a snack. The innkeeper, a beefy Greek in a brown chlamys with the face of a bouncer, which he probably was as well, told him that there were a couple of ships in the port that would leave for Alexandria in a day or two.

"I have a room on the second floor available if you need a place to stay," he added.

"Yes, keep it for me, will you?" Nil answered and added a couple more coins as an advance.

"Sure thing," the innkeeper said and pocketed the coins. "You will find the ship in the port. She's a small sailing vessel with a few oars to maneuver in a harbor and a single deck. The whole crew is about a dozen people. I think they've got a load of fine woolen fabric here and hope to sell it in Alexandria. You know, there is not many buyers around here in Judea since Albinus became a procurator. The people are poor and Alexandria is rich, so they hope to sell there with profit. You will need a boat to get to the ship. There are always plenty of boatmen there ready to ferry you to the ship for a couple of leptons. Don't pay more than a brass semis for the roundtrip."

"Thanks," Nil said. "I'll go now."

"You know, you don't have to," the innkeeper said. "Her captain, Jason, is going to come here soon anyway. He has to pick up a small parcel with spices that I am sending to my partner in Alexandria. I am sure he'll be happy to get a passenger; they barely make ends meet in their business."

Nil shrugged his shoulders and sat back. After all, the sun was almost set and searching in the harbor for captains who were most likely already sitting in the taverns on the shore, did not look like an attractive way to spend the time to him.

"Sure, then bring me some food and wine, and I will wait for him," Nil said. "Some cheese and bread would be nice, and splash some oil on the bottom of the plate to go with the bread."

"I have a balsamic vinegar from Crete," the innkeeper said and his gloomy face lit with an almost happy smile. "It gives a very nice touch to the oil."

"Sure, sounds good," Nil said. Apparently, he is not just the innkeeper and the bouncer, Nil decided, the guy is also a gourmet. A great skill set for the tavern keeper. Anyway, it does not matter as long as he is right about this captain.

The innkeeper was right. Captain Jason, a sturdy built, bearded Greek, about forty years old, came to the tavern in about half an hour. He exchanged a few words with the innkeeper, and then joined Nil in his corner.

"I was told you are looking for a fare to Alexandria. Is that right?" he said while inspecting Nil's face and dress. "My name is Jason, and my ship is going to Alexandria tomorrow morning."

"Yes, that's correct," Nil said. "My name is Nil. Consider taking a passenger?"

"Ten pieces of silver and consider yourself already in Alexandria," Jason said.

"Ten denarii for a couple of days trip? Are you looking for an early retirement?" Nil asked. "I could buy your whole ship for that money."

"No, you can not," Jason said, smiling from ear to ear, and sat in front of Nil. "You need at least four times more. Just for you, eight pieces of silver and we will deliver you like fresh flowers for the Egyptian queen's court."

"Three," Nil said and grinned lightly. "I am not a flower and Egypt does not have a queen."

"You have a point," Jason laughed and stroke his beard. "Fine, five and your own food. We'll take care of drinking water. Come on, you probably can get this covered by the paymaster when you get to your legion."

He probably took me for a simple legionnaire following to the place of service, Nil realized. I could probably press the price down a bit more, but why bother? The price is fair and he is right, it will be covered, so why not.

"Pay upon delivery?"

"Three now, two in Alexandria," Jason said and nodded to the innkeeper. "Otus knows me, I always do my end of the deal."

"Yes, he does," Otus confirmed, appearing nearby with a couple of empty mugs in his hands that he was cleaning. "Half of his crew are those Christians. They don't even let him rob other ships. That's on the rare occasions when he can, of course. Not that he can rob many on his trough anyway," he said with a grin.

"You have a deal," Nil said. "Care for some wine? Be my guest."

"Just a mug to sprinkle the deal," Jason said. "I still have a bunch of things to do before departure."

He grabbed a mug from Otus's hand, filled it from the pitcher, and knocked the contents down his throat in a single swing. Nil hardly had time enough to prepare the money he agreed to pay.

"See you tomorrow in the port before daybreak. My ship is in the far south corner. Just tell the boatmen to get you to Captain Jason's *Tehe* – the name means "luck" – they know my ship. Or, even better, I'll ask somebody from my crew to pick you up here at the inn and show the way. Don't be late, we sail away at dawn."

He waved his hand and left.

"A very decent man," Otus said while picking up the empty mug. "Why is it always decent men who are poor, and scum gets rich?"

Nil recalled his meeting with the procurator and sadly shrugged his shoulders.

"That's what I think too," Otus said with a nod. "About sending a man to show you the way to the ship, that's his way of saying thanks for the little extra you agreed to pay. You know, he could probably agree to four pieces, and I noticed, you saw that. You are not an accidental profit for him now, you are a passenger."

"How long will it take to get to Alexandria?" Nil asked. "The Cap'n did not mention that."

"Of course he did not," Otus said. "The sailors are superstitious. He's probably prayed in the local temples of sea and wind gods, not to mention asking his crew to pray for good weather to whoever they believe in. You know, just in case. With a favorable wind you should be in place in a couple of days, just like you said yourself."

* * *

The sky was already light when *Tehe's* crewmember brought Nil to the place in the port. The ship was anchored about half a mile away from the shore, but, courtesy of Captain Jason, a boatman was waiting to deliver them to the ship. The sun had not shown up yet, but a shining golden line emphasized the horizon, adding to the dim light of the early dawn. The smell of rotting fish was thick in the air, as this part of the port was mostly used by fishing boats rather than cargo ships.

The ship appeared to be a small trade vessel with almost identical stern and bow, no ram, no deck – Otus was exaggerating when describing the vessel – and a single removable mast. It was much smaller than *Glapos*, a little more than a dozen paces in length and about four paces in width. Large width made the vessel more steady. It also allowed the captain to load more cargo, although that made the ship slower and less maneuverable. On the plus side, the nine crewmembers including the captain – Otus exaggerated that too – were quite enough to handle the ship.

Nil got on board, and they cast off. At first, when the crew was rowing out of the harbor, everybody was busy. So Nil just laid down at the bow, where he did not interfere with anybody, wrapped himself in his cloak and considered taking a nap time. In less than a quarter of an hour, the crew got the ship into the open sea, set a rectangular sail, and then most of them, except the helmsman at the stern and a man on watch, followed Nil's example.

Unfortunately, you can only sleep for so much. So in a few hours almost everybody woke up and was busy doing nothing.

"Good weather," Nil said to the captain, who stood up at the bow leaning on the board.

"Yeah, low waves and a good wind in the right direction," Jason said. "Seems that we are lucky so far."

"Otus said we may be there in two days," Nil said. "Sounds right?"

"Well, let's not scare off our luck," Jason said. "Sea is deceptive. If gods favor us, we may be there as Otus said. I'd rather add no more."

"Speaking of gods," Nil said. "Otus said you have a lot of Christians in your crew."

"Sure, I have," Jason said. "Zeno! Come here."

One of the crew members got to his feet and walked carefully to Nil and the captain.

"Zeno, this is the man from Rome," Jason said. "His name is Nil, and he wanted to meet a Christian. He never met one before."

Zeno looked at Nil, the silent question on his face.

"Actually, I have," Nil said with quiet dignity and crossed his fingers in a special way he learned when working with Roman Christians. "I just was surprised to hear that our communities go so far to the East."

"And I am pleasantly surprised that our communities go so far to the West," Zeno said with a light bow of the head. "How are things going in Rome?"

"Not so well," Nil said. "But maybe we should go to the stern and not bother the captain with our affairs."

"Sure, go ahead" Jason said to Zeno. "You know I am not interested, and I don't mind if you discuss your secrets a bit. There is not much to do now anyway."

Nil and Zeno moved to the aft of the ship near the helmsman. Two other sailors free of duty joined them.

"You may speak freely with them," Zeno said, pointing to the sailors and the helmsman. "They are all our brothers. What is it that bothers you?"

"Bad news is heard in Rome," Nil said. "It looks like some of our brothers will try a huge arson in Rome sometime in the autumn."

"Why would they do that?" Zeno asked.

"They believe it's a time foretold by prophets when Rome will be destroyed," Nil said. "And they want to be a part of it."

"This is really sad news," one of the sailors said. "The empire has not liked us so far, but if something like that happens–"

"They will crush us," Zeno finished. "Truly sad news you brought to us, Brother Nil. But what can we do?"

"Talk to your communities, discourage them from participating in it," Nil said. "And keep an eye on those who will."

"Don't worry about our communities, brother," Zeno said. "We are all poor people, most of us don't have the means to travel to Rome nor the time to do so. Of course, we will talk to them anyway. As for keeping an eye out, who are they, those insane people who are planning such a crime?"

"Their leader's name is Benjamin," Nil said. "He is a trader going around between Egypt, Judea, Crete, Greece and Italy. Sometimes he tries to look like a prophet who just foretells the destruction of Rome, but as the people begin to listen, he calls for actually doing it."

"We will keep an eye out for such a man," Zeno nodded. "And we will warn the communities that we visit."

"But what can we do with him?" one of the sailors asked. "We can't give him up to the authorities, he is one of our brothers."

"Of course, we can't," Nil said. "That's why it is so important to find him and try to deal with him on our own before he makes all of us hunted animals. If you see him or hear about him, try to pass a word to me in Rome. Find the house of the prefect of Praetorians Guards. There is a man named Alexius there – he will know how to pass the word to me."

"Prefect's house?" Zeno asked, raising his brows.

"Yes," Nil said. "We are in many places around Rome. Alexius teaches rhetoric to the prefect's children. He is a freedman, but this is a good job. Besides, who knows, maybe he will be able to teach them not just rhetoric?"

"This sounds like good news," Zeno agreed. "It's joyous to hear that our community in Rome prospers and reaches so deep there. We will try to let you know. None of our brothers go regularly to Rome, but we may have an occasion here and there.

Or we can find a seaman going there who will be willing to pass the word for a few coins."

"Thank you," Nil said and gave a light bow. Damn, he thought, it's really a pity that I cannot instruct them to use the Imperial post.

"Thank you for the word of caution," Zeno said politely. "That's our common burden."

"Do you think Benjamin may get many people for his plot here in the East?" Nil asked.

"I doubt that," Zeno said with a shake of his head. "As I said already, most of us are poor people who cannot go around at will. Few of our brothers around may be imprudent enough to revolt, if the life becomes too hard, but conspiracy like that? No, that requires some money."

BROTHERS IN CHRIST, SMILE!
Chapter XIV, where we learn how to expose Christians in their own words

A young dark haired man, a little older than twenty, walked in the last rays of the evening sun along the narrow Roman street away from Palatine Hill. He was shorter than average and his puny constitution made some of the people on the street grin at him. His rare beard and moustache contrasted with the shaved faces of Romans, while his Semitic features distinguished him from Greeks, who also often had a predilection for keeping their face hair. He was dressed in a loin-cloth and a rectangular piece of fabric he threw over his shoulders like a simple cloak, covering a few pieces of papyrus that he kept pressed to his chest as a most treasured possession. His *soleae* sandals were basically a pair of soles kept on the foot with a couple of laces. The "cloak" did not belong to him, it was given for going out to the city by the chief supervisor of the household who patronized the young man. Technically, neither did the loin-cloth, sandals, or even himself. The young man was a slave. The only thing that really belonged to him was written on the pieces of papyrus that the teacher gave him.

Benjamin, the servant in Tigellinus' house, was not exactly cleaning the toilets. He supervised toilet cleaning by other slaves – which was much cleaner and a more appropriate occupation for an orthodox Jew. Technically, as the slaves had little choice in the job line, there would not be much dishonor for him even if he was to actually clean the toilets, but being in almost constant contact with unclean substances would be considered a serious drawback for leading the righteous life. Anyway, his aspirations were to become free again some day and, maybe, enter some decent profession like one of a scribe. And as the first step, he hoped to move to a more decent job as a slave.

He had all the chances for that. Literate slaves were rare, and the ability to both read, write, and count put him above a lot of them. In fact, that's how he got his current position. The chief supervisor of the house – Tigellinus did not bother himself with such earthly details – did not want to waste a literate slave on a primitive job and instead made him a supervisor with the potential for a better job, if Benjamin was able to prove himself.

Benjamin certainly tried. The example of patriarch Joseph, who was a slave once and rose to become the second to the King of Egypt himself, gave him the inspiration to struggle with everyday routine. Who knows, he thought, maybe he can get a better assignment, then even better, and eventually rise to the top of the household hierarchy. And after he becomes a freed man, he would still be around the master, his trusted man. Praetorians had a lot of influence in Rome, so the master could raise in status even more some time in the future and become the king or, how they call it here, the emperor. After all, freed men of the current emperor are all around with important jobs to do and a decent income to enjoy. Why cannot this happen to me, thought Benjamin, dreaming about the future.

And he did not just dream. He was looking around, trying to figure out how the life around him worked, and what to do to rise among others. The house of a rich Roman was very similar to a large bureaucratic organization, with its feuds, alliances, politics, battles, victories, and losses around small items like favors of supervisors, better assignments, influence, or even simply a piece of food. The most ambitious ones were competing for the favors of the chief supervisor – a freed man set to supervise the household. Fighting for the favors of the master himself – Tigellinus – was unthinkable. Only "high priests" among the slaves were allowed into the holiest of holies – the master's bedroom or a triclinium – when he cared to dine at home. Which he usually did not.

This lack of a big picture and vision in other slaves encouraged Benjamin to think that he may succeed in getting the top prize – the favor of the master himself. He knew that excelling in his current assignment would not bring him closer to this goal by itself. However, neglecting it would definitely block any hope, so he paid good attention to his job and was praised on many occasions by the chief supervisor himself. Excellence in his job made his name mentioned around, and he knew how important it was to be on everybody's mind just in case that rare opportunity strikes.

It had worked out well so far. Once the master had need of expert advice about the Jewish traditions and existing sects.

There were not many Jewish slaves in Rome, but there were a few in Tigellinus' household. Benjamin knew whom to thank for being chosen among them to talk to the master. In fact, he did thank the chief supervisor. He saved a few coins from the occasional bonuses given to him, and bought a lucky charm in one of the pagan temples crowding Rome. Giving money would be a very stupid idea, as first, he did not possess enough money to interest the chief supervisor, and second, all the money he had, he was given by the chief supervisor himself. But a lucky charm of the supervisor's family deity, with a portion of thanks and praises for his benevolence, wisdom, and knowledge of the household, apparently touched this usually harsh and cruel man and ensured that Benjamin would be remembered the next time the master needed a talk with one of his slaves.

From the one, and so far the only, conversation with the master, Benjamin understood that he did not have a soft spot for Christians, the object of despise of the Roman Jewish community. In fact, Tigellinus openly disliked them. So now Benjamin's primary hopes were with the book. Yes, "the book", that's how Benjamin thought of it. Being an orthodox Jew, he aspired to make his name remembered by writing a book that would depict the Christians as heretics for what he thought they really were, showing their vile deeds and thoughts. The central point of the book was supposed to be about a Christian conspiracy to burn and destroy Jerusalem in their envy of righteous people.

The signed pieces of papyrus contained the first pages of the book that he was going to give to his teacher of Law. Doctor ben-Ata Khin was a respected scholar who successfully combined his study of Law with a flourishing dental practice that gave him a good income and the time for his studies. His income was so good that he could afford a house – the luxury most of the people born and raised in Rome could not afford for their entire life.

The teacher took him to his study room, a small premise crowded with a desk, a chair, a bench, and hardly any space to move around them. The small window on top of the outer wall was giving some light but overall the room looked somewhat dark after the sunny street. Doctor ben-Ata sat in the chair and pointed to the bench that was set there specially for disciples.

"First, tell me how your work and position in the house of the prefect is going," ben-Ata said in their native tongue.

"I have not had a chance to talk to the master again," Benjamin said. "However, I enjoy the favorable disposition of the chief supervisor. He praised me twice today, and he gave me this piece of cloth to cover my body when going to the city."

"Glad to hear that, my boy," the teacher said. "Remember, you should do your duties diligently and always look for a chance to show yourself as a trustworthy and hardworking man."

"I will, teacher," Benjamin said.

"Now, read it to me, my boy," ben-Ata said. "My eyes are not as sharp these days as they used to be."

"Should I read in our language or the Greek translation?" Benjamin asked. He wrote everything in Aramaic, but also translated it to Greek as the teacher instructed him.

"Ours, of course," ben-Ata smiled paternally at the young man.

"Let me start from the instructions of the Christian archbishop to the ones who will go set fire to Jerusalem," Benjamin said and started to read. "Brothers in Christ! Smile when entering the city and the houses that you are going to burn. Remember, you are doing the bidding of our Lord, Jesus, the God of Christians, and when you are seized and executed, you will join our Lord and get the reward for your deeds. Don't hesitate when you see children or women on the streets and in the houses, as truly this is an evil city and evil people, and there is no measure of the hate that our Lord keeps for these people and this city. When the sun sets, throw your torches to the windows, and don't let others put out the fire. When you see a vessel with oil, break it so that the fire can go wild, cleansing the abominations of this city and these people. Rejoice as fire will start consuming the city as you are doing a blessed job and your souls will join our Lord in Heavens, not like those perishing in fire, who repelled him..."

He read for some time until the teacher raised his hand with a sign to stop.

"I see that you tried, but –" the teacher shook his head, sighed, then continued. "But, Benjamin, you missed all I told you last time. Your text sounds like they are really right, and we are really wrong. How can you do it this way?"

"But, teacher," Benjamin said, "won't they represent it exactly this way, so that they look good and we look bad?"

"They? Could be," the teacher said. "But that's not the point. Do you want to act like these unclean traitors do, or do you want to act as a righteous man? Then why do it like they would do? You see how much more powerful your message may be if these traitors, the Christians, expose themselves in their own words?"

"But teacher," Benjamin asked, "why would they expose themselves?"

"I see you have more faith in those heretics than in your teacher," ben-Ata said and sighed again.

"No, teacher, I trust you," Benjamin said. "It's just I am lost and cannot grasp your wisdom so quickly. Can you show me what you mean?"

"Of course," ben-Ata smiled at him. "See, you wrote 'evil city', 'blessed job', that's not right. You need to say something like, 'when entering Jerusalem, that blessed city of righteous, whom we envy, feel your vile joy as you are going to set them on fire.' You see, this way their own words betray them. By the way, did you notice that you never called Jerusalem by name? You see, you are writing this not only to Jews, but also to Greeks and Romans. How would they know what city you are talking about?"

"I see, teacher," Benjamin said. "Yes, I will rewrite it as you advise."

"Good, good," ben-Ata nodded, saying that. "Now take more papyrus and show me something better next time. You are a good student, Benjamin. Make me proud of you."

It was already dark when Benjamin left his teacher's house. The streets were empty, and he mentally thanked the chief-supervisor again for the piece of fabric that kept him from the evening cool air. He hurried up along the street, turned around the corner, and stumbled upon three vigils. Vigils were Roman firemen and the night watch organized by districts and looking for order in the city, helping the city cohorts and praetorians. The eldest vigil frowned. Benjamin, hiding the manuscript under the improvised cloak, raised suspicions in him.

"Who are you?" he asked.

"Benjamin, your honor, a slave. I have to get to the house of my master soon or my supervisor will be very angry at me."

"And what are you doing around so late?"

"I was outside on an errand," Benjamin said. He decided that it would be safer to lie a bit as these people would clearly not be too sympathetic toward a slave late from his time off in the city.

"And what do you have here?" the vigil asked.

"Just a few pieces of papyrus, your honor," Benjamin said. "Please, let me go, your honor. I really must get home in time or the supervisor will punish me."

"Follow us," the vigil ordered and turned to his fellows. "Let's get him to the quarters, boys, and see what the boss says. You remember how a month ago we got a slave who was hurrying up just like this one? He happened to be at large for three months."

Benjamin obeyed and they walked down the street. Fortunately, the quarters were close enough because vigils were stationed in individual districts, not in the Praetorian camp in the northern part of the city. They walked uneventfully in the empty streets for less than half an hour until they arrived. Vigils quarters in this district were located in a two-story house with a wide front yard. The one in charge nodded in the direction of an old cart and said, "Sit here."

Benjamin sat in the cart and waited for the situation to clear out.

"Lupis!" the vigil shouted, looking at the lit window on the second floor.

"What?" the voice from behind the window answered.

"We've got a slave who was hurrying to his master's house in the dark," the vigil said.

"And why the hell did you bring him here?" the voice answered. "Deal him a blow and let him run home."

The vigil, without hesitation, cuffed Benjamin on the nape and said, "Get out!"

Benjamin, without lingering for a second invitation, picked up the papyrus, and ran away. After the second corner, he stopped to catch his breath and looked at the manuscript. The original version of the archbishop's instructions both in Hebrew and Greek was gone. Oh, well, he thought, the clean sheets are with him, and the teacher said to get rid of the original version anyway. So he pressed the papyrus to his chest and hurried on home.

"Brothers in Christ! Smile when entering the city and the houses that you are going to burn..." were the first words in Greek and Hebrew on two pieces of papyrus left in the yard of the vigils, in a cart confiscated from some Greek trader three months ago and used as a support for hay. "BNJMN" was inscribed in Aramaic letters on the back of each piece.

LOCAL STINKERS DON'T COUNT
Chapter XV, where one Roman, one Greek, and one Egyptian are looking for one Christian Jew and cannot find him

Nothing else noteworthy happened in the two final days that Nil spent with Captain Jason and his crew. He talked a couple more times to Zeno and his men, made sure that they knew where to pass word if they learned something about the trader Benjamin, and spent the rest of the time sleeping and staring at the horizon and the shoreline.

A silhouette of the Pharos lighthouse – the huge three-story tower showing the entrance to the harbor – was growing slowly in front of their eyes as they were closing on the city at the end of the second day. The ancient land greeted them with one of its man-made miracles that was famed across the Roman world. Beside the lighthouse, the entrance to the harbor was also surrounded by two temples of Isis, the great goddess of Egypt. One occupied the closest, eastward, part of the island between the lighthouse and an artificial dam connecting the island with the mainland. Another one was located on Cape Lochias, that came into the sea right between the Jewish and Royal quarters of the city and enclosed the harbor from the east.

Both complexes were clearly seen in the crisp air of the dying day. A vast rectangular area was surrounded by walls and included the main edifice and a spacious square divided into a number of areas, each with its special purpose. Somewhat similar to the Jerusalem temple, Nil thought, looking at the massive structures over the board. Compared to them, the magnificent-by-itself Greek temple of Poseidon on the farthest corner of the island looked lightweight because of its graceful Corinthian columns and wide arcs.

It's not Roman, Nil realized. The cult of Isis was permitted in Rome and it had there a temple as well as numerous followers, including a few of Nil's acquaintances. The Roman temple of Isis was a temple, all right. Rich, impressive, just like the temples of Jupiter, Venus, Minerva, or many other numerous deities fancied in the city of cities. It featured few exotic ceremonies and was surrounded by some special mystic aura, but now Nil realized that it was Roman in essence, just spiced and flavored a bit differently. Compared to *that*, Nil thought, the temple in Rome looked like a fake. He looked at the massive rectangular structures that erupted from the ground and breathed with the primordial power of the Earth itself, and the idea that the priests of this goddess can engulf the huge city in flames did not look so fantastic and ridiculous anymore. He knew that these were places he would have to pay a visit soon.

The harbor was busy this time of the year. The large ships were loaded with Egyptian grain and sailing to Italy. While they were closing on the city, two large ships left the harbor and turned West away from them along the North African coast. Granary ships relied on sails, and with predominantly opposite winds it could take a month or two for them to reach Ostia, the main port of Rome. Anyway, the harbor was too busy with the things really important to the empire to accept an insignificant boat with a few smugglers. Nil was pretty sure that Captain Jason was not going to declare his merchandise in the port or pay customs, even if any were due, but saw no reason to intervene. In fact, a smuggler who trusts you could be a great source of information, Nil thought, and Captain Jason looked like a good candidate to work with.

Anyway, the intentions of the port authorities and the captain were aligned almost perfectly. The former did not want to deal with an insignificant vessel, and the latter wanted to avoid them dealing with it. So Jason moved east of the harbor to the Jewish quarter of the city. The sun had not yet set when the ship touched the sandy sea bottom and got firmly beached among the stinking fishing boats returning home after the day. The crew jumped out and anchored the vessel to make sure that the leaving high water would not pull it back to sea, so Nil stepped on the land without getting his feet wet. He thanked the captain, paid him the rest of the fare, and left to the city after saying goodbye to all four Christian members of the crew.

What simpletons, Nil thought going down the street toward the port. They trusted me on the spot and promised to send a note directly to the prefect's house. Besides, it looks like they were more scared of the prospect that some of their "brothers" are going to burn Rome than the prefect himself. *I wonder, Nil's thoughts had switched to Tigellinus, where the boss found this information in the first place. In his place, I would triple check such information before believing it. Sure, something is brewing around, but the more I go to the East, the fewer the traces of conspiracy. Looks like it's all centered around Rome. Zeno was right,* he thought, *a conspiracy like this takes some money.*

A place to stay and eat was not a problem in Alexandria. Ubiquitous Greeks felt at home here, which was easy to understand, keeping in mind that Egypt was ruled by Greeks for several centuries since Alexander the Great. They opened a lot of taverns and inns around the city. And, as of little surprise, most of them were close to the port.

Egypt was ruled by a prefect. He had several procurators on his staff who supervised financial matters and, with special attention, the grain shipments to Rome. He also had a few other officials reporting to him, including military commanders, a legal advisor, *iuridicus*, the chief priest, *idios logos* who supervised and accounted for tax collection, and a few others. Besides them, there was a number of officials on the regional level and in each *nom*, an administrative unit of Egypt usually centered around some city. Through military commanders, the prefect directly controlled the legions stationed in the province. In a sense, the prefect was as powerful as pharaohs of the older days, except that frequent – once every several years – replacements made it complicated to deify the prefect and consider him an earthly incarnation of some god. The latter was mended somewhat by deifying the current emperor, whom the prefect officially represented. It was not as good for Egyptians as "a god next door", which they were accustomed to for a few millennia, but it was the next best thing and, besides, nobody cared much about what Egyptians thought anyway.

Nil got an audience with the current prefect – Lucius Julius Vistinus – the next day. *It certainly pays to carry documents signed by the prefect of Praetorians,* Nil thought. *God-like or not, but all these provincial rulers hope to get back to Rome one day with money and influence, and they don't want to be at odds with one of the most powerful men in the city.*

The palace was located on the east side of the harbor in the Royal, actually Greek, quarter of the city. It was surrounded by a garden enclosed by a high wall with guarded entrances, and the main gate accompanied by two steles of red granite called "Cleopatra needles". The prefect listened to Nil *tête-à-tête* in a private back room of his palace. Lucius Julius Vistinus was in his mid sixties. He had already been the prefect of Egypt for five years and handled the job well. Combining both civilian and military powers, he did not wear a toga, but rather light armor over a white tunic complemented by a short red military cloak for going out, which now rested on the back of a chair. Not that the weather required a cloak, on the contrary it was rather hot outside, but status was more important. Besides, the light linen protected the armor from getting hot under the burning southern sun.

"More trouble from those Jews," the prefect said after Nil finished. "I am going to meet the chief priest tomorrow morning. He is also the high priest of the temple of Isis on the island so he is always missing when I need him. Anyway, come here and meet him. He will assign some of his deputies to assist you on the case. You probably want to visit the temples located in the city, at least the major Egyptian ones. I'll assign one of my men to accompany you and confirm your credentials to them. I think, that's it. I have not heard anything about this trader Benjamin, nor anything about the arson plans. But I'll alert my men to be on the lookout."

After Nil left, a thin and short man, about sixty years old, in a white toga on top of an off-white tunic, came into the room. His face, covered with red spots and bluish veins on the temples, kept obliging expressions although not without a hint of the hidden arrogance of a servant confided with the master's most dirty and dangerous secrets. A bald spot covering the top of his head and deep large wrinkles made him look like a large dog, indifferent to the world while ready to follow his master's orders expressed with a simple move of a finger. In other words, this was a man one would expect near a capable ruler.

"Did you hear him, Galen?" the prefect asked. "What do you think?"

"Yes, I've heard it all," Galen said. "It sounds very strange. If you don't mind, I'd like to be the one assigned to this man to help with his investigation. Even assuming there is a link between that sect and some Egyptian temples, why would the priests help in such an endeavor? They have absolutely nothing to benefit from it."

"True," the prefect nodded. "Still, I wonder if we should be prepared in case this fire actually happens. I hate to be caught off guard by unexpected events."

"Of course, but I don't believe we have any preparations to make," the man said. "Nothing to worry about anyway."

"What do you mean?" the prefect asked.

"There certainly will be some changes," Galen answered. "The price of grain will go up, hence better profits. There will be a need for expedient shipping, hence a chance to distinguish yourself. A lot of Egyptian stone will be required to rebuild Rome. The rumors from travelers from Rome are that the emperor is not very happy with his palace. He calls it *Domus Transitoria* – passage-through house. Not a very flattering name for the emperor's residence. So I suspect that the red granite of Aswan will be required in large quantities. And if the fire is serious enough, you may be able to secure a spot in a good location for your future house. You know, after you leave this post, return to Rome, and retire."

"You see?" the prefect said. "There is a lot to prepare. Expedient shipping may require a few spare ships in the harbor at the time. Increasing production of red granite cannot be done overnight. It's better to have some reserve ready when the emperor requests it. And I should think about a nice spot in Rome where I can build my house, after the place becomes available."

"That's only in case," Galen said politely, "Rome does burn."

"You are right," the prefect said. "Spare ships are an expensive thing, and there is no sense looking for a spot if it will not be freed by the fire."

He looked to the mosaic ceiling and paused, thinking. Galen did not interrupt, waiting politely for his boss. The noise of the city did not penetrate the garden around the palace. The silence was only interrupted by the light rustle of foliage under the breeze and the birds singing in the tree crones outside. After a few minutes, the prefect turned his attention back to his man. "Do you think we can trust those Jews with something so important?"

"Can you trust Jews with anything?" Galen grinned.

* * *

The next morning Nil came to the palace again. This time the reception was in a hall. Not the big hall for official ceremonies, but a smaller, private one, still suitable for several men to talk far enough from the walls that could have uninvited ears.

Akenisis, the chief priest in the Roman administration of Egypt and the High Priest of Isis, came accompanied by a self-confident man in his early fifties with the tenacious grip of his dark brown eyes. Both were dressed in chlamys-style dress on top of embroidered kilts held with multicolored belts and traditional Egyptian headpieces covering their hair.

After entering the hall, Akenisis slowly and stately turned, looking at the prefect who waited standing in the middle of the hall with crossed arms. Very old, in his late seventies, but not decrepit, the priest looked like an ancient king visiting his worthless pawns with an inspection. He was so bony that one could not dismiss the thought that he really could be an ancient king woken up from one of the numerous tombs in the southern dessert, but the arrogant, greedy and very vivid look of his eyes provided proof to the contrary.

"The old ape puffs up," the prefect muttered, looking at the priest. "Dear Akenisis, glad to see you," he said loudly. "Do you mind coming closer so that we can talk?" Then he lowered his voice again and said to Nil, "See the second man? You will work with him. He is the head of the temple police under this dressed monkey."

The priest bowed slightly and approached the prefect in the same slow and stately fashion as he was standing before. His companion followed him one step behind.

"Simaat, good to see you!" the prefect said, looking at the priest's companion. "Dear Akeni, you brought the right man for our riddle today; we will need his help."

"What can we do for mighty Rome?" the priest asked.

"Nil, tell them."

And Nil started his story again. Simaat, the priest's companion, listened attentively, and though he looked relaxed, Nil was sure that he did not miss a single word or any detail. In contrast, the priest was neither relaxed, nor attentive. He probably missed most of what Nil said, but he got what mattered to him – there is a conspiracy and his people are suspected in it.

"I never heard of anything like this before," the priest said.

"Sure, you did not," the prefect said. "If you did, you would inform me, right? Now, I want you to help with the investigation of what you may have not heard yet, but what may be there."

"Let Simaat help with the investigation," the priest said. "If there is anything, he will find it."

"I could not agree more, dear Akeni," the prefect said. "Now before we get to the other temple matters, let's dismiss our investigators. They have a job to do." He turned away from the priest and said, "Simaat, Nil is on a personal mission from the prefect of Praetorians in Rome, help him with the investigation. You've heard the problem. Anyway, you two are professionals – you will find a way to work this out. Grab Galen on the way out; he will help you too, especially if you need my authority. Galen will keep me informed." He turned to Nil. "Come to me before leaving Egypt, I will need a detailed report on your investigation. Go."

Nil and Simaat left the hall. Galen was already waiting outside.

They looked at each other. It was hard to read anything from the firm and expressionless look in Simaat's eyes. Self-confident, experienced, dangerous, Nil decided, and on my side. Then he looked at the other man. That must be Galen, the appointee of the prefect, Nil decided. Experienced, greedy, no principles, dangerous, Nil thought. Hey, what's the matter, I am not a little baby myself.

"I need to be off now. I need to warn my men to be on the lookout for this Benjamin of yours," Simaat said. "Tomorrow morning let us visit local temples, Roman."

There was no hate in the way he said "Roman", neither was there any piety. I like him, Nil thought, while Simaat turned and walked away.

"He is ok, even though a little too Egyptian," Galen said with a grin. "Let's meet tomorrow morning one hour after daybreak at the tavern of old Amphion. Let me show you where it is. We can get some drinks there, and talk about our business too, while our colleague warns his men. Actually, later today I'll alert my boys too."

And you are a little too Greek, Nil thought, but that's ok.

"Sounds like a plan," he said with a wide smile.

* * *

The next few days were busy. Nil, Galen, and Simaat were visiting the city temples devoted to multiple Egyptian deities. The city had an abundance of both temples and deities. The head priests of the temples were shaking their heads, promising to look for any followers of Benjamin who might try to approach them, but otherwise were clueless. Not everybody cooperated at once, but Galen and Simaat knew the city, the people, and how to make a person cooperate without touching him with a finger. Still, no traces were found.

Nil felt desperate. This was the core of his assignment, and it did not work out. If Egyptian priests are not involved, then it seemed like he was wrong all along. What's even worse, he had no clue who could be at the heart of such a grand-scale conspiracy. At last, the third priest of the Temple of *Amun-Ra*, who was noticed talking to a Greek trader a month ago, gave them a hint. The trader himself happened to be a provider of a certain spice bought for the needs of the Temple, and so it was a false alarm. But after listening to the story, the priest gave them an idea.

"You are looking for the real Egyptian priests, not the local puff-ups," he said. The man was old and visibly unconcerned with his own well-being. "Alexandria is all about the power, not the faith. Nobody serves gods here, everybody serves himself, maybe Romans. If you look for power, you go to Alexandria, if you look for ancient sacred knowledge, you go to Heliopolis."

"I thought Heliopolis is a Greek city," Nil said. "It certainly sounds like a Greek city."

The old man smiled.

"He may have some point," Galen said. "Alexandria is all about politics and power plays. You would not believe, we cannot handle all the reports that people place against each other. We had one man whose house is free from taxation. Last year we got thirty seven reports on him as hiding his house from taxes. All voluntary, all from good friends and neighbors. It's not easy to keep any real knowledge in such a place. Thebes, the old capital of Egypt, may keep some secrets and dangerous knowledge."

The old man smiled again.

"Thebes declined since Alexandria was built," Simaat said. "But Memphis is our old capital, their priests may be involved."

The old man sighed without saying anything.

"Speak," Nil demanded.

"Before Alexandria was Thebes," the priest said. "Before Thebes was Memphis. But before both of them, before Romans and Greeks, several waves of Greeks, even before Egypt was united, there was *On* – our ancient spiritual capital called *Iunu* or *Per-Ra* in our ancient scripts. You call it Heliopolis. Go there. If you do not find your answers there, you will not find them anywhere in Egypt."

"What do you think?" Nil asked when all three investigators left the temple.

"The old man may be right," Simaat said. "I have to admit, the priests here in Alexandria are mere mortals with little pleasures of life and little sins of their own. The top of their ambitions is to get to the top here and become a chief priest, and those are the ones who have any ambitions at all. They are not fit for something as grand as you described. And he is right – Thebes and Memphis have both declined significantly. They probably hardly recognize Rome's existence at all. No, if something is brewing around, that should be in On. They keep there our ancient knowledge and they are the only ones who may be capable of doing something serious."

"Yeah, I agree, the local stinkers don't count," Galen said, ignoring the indignant glance from Simaat. "Hey, no offense, you would not try to burn Rome even if you could, right? You depend on us to keep your power and you have nothing to gain from it. And besides, you don't know how to do it."

"Arrogant as it's said," Simaat said with dignity. "I have to admit, your words have a grain of truth in them. No matter the connections, we have nothing to gain from such a plan. And I doubt that any priest from Alexandria is predisposed to participate in any risky enterprise on a charitable basis. And even if offered significant money, nobody would be able to implement such a plan."

TRUST THE LORD
Chapter XVI, where Gessimus Florus gets a province, and Bin Jamen a.k.a. Nil gets a ghostwriter

It was the first day of *Lemuria*, the feast of dead. Rome was unusually quiet in the evening. Well, not really quiet. Rome is never quiet. However, compared to the usual night rumpus, it was quiet this night. The emperor was sober. Well, almost. You would not expect him to keep this up for all nine days of Lemuria, but getting drunk on the very first day would certainly look inappropriate. Getting girls did not seem like an appropriate idea either, at least for now. Maybe later. For now the emperor had fun listening to the reports from the provinces that Tigellinus read to him aloud.

They were reclining on couches in a small triclinium in the back of the palace specially designed for confidential or private meetings. The room had four couches and a table in the middle. The walls were covered by heavy deep-green drapery, hiding a couple of niches behind them. Several oil lamps were lighting the place. Two couches were vacant; the emperor and Tigellinus were alone in the room. Again, almost alone – there was a couple of slaves serving wine and food. Yes, wine. If you remember, the emperor was *almost* sober.

"Here is a report from my man in Judea," Tigellinus said. "That's the one who investigates the threat of an arson in September."

"Go on," the emperor said, taking another bunch of southern Italian grape. He was bored, but a languor all over his body felt pleasant and relaxing, so he just continued to do nothing. With this soothing apathy filling him, listening to the reports was sort of fun. Not that they contained anything interesting, but they did not distract thoughts from roaming elsewhere either.

"He writes that he found the traces of that Benjamin somewhere near Caesarea," Tigellinus said, "but neither the procurator nor Judean authorities are aware of them."

"Benjamin?" the emperor asked.

"Yes, that one, you remember," Tigellinus said. "Oh, yes, Bin Jamen."

"Oh, that one," the emperor said. "So he really has become a traitor if you need to send other people to catch him."

"Eh?" Tigellinus said. "Oh, yes, Caesar, he did!"

Nil, you lucky bastard, Tigellinus thought. If you'd know that Caesar just turned your death sentence onto that mysterious Greek trader you are chasing after. Tigellinus chuckled aloud at his thoughts.

"What's so funny?" the emperor asked.

"He reports that Jews are ready to revolt at any moment," Tigellinus said, covering his thoughts. "And he says that only Albinus' wise rule keeps them under control."

"Wise rule?" the emperor laughed. "So funny. Did they send levy in time this year?"

"Yes, Caesar, they did," Tigellinus said.

"Speaking of levies and September arson," the emperor's thoughts clearly steered away from Judea. "Do you think it's ridiculous that we will only make money on oil, but not on the grain if this fire happens? After all, Rome consumes ten times more grain than oil."

"Yes," Tigellinus agreed. "But you remember what Galba said. We need a war or a revolt somewhere close to Egypt to make money on grain—"

He broke off. Apathy washed away from the faces of both men. They looked at each other in a silent surprise.

"Do you think Judea is close enough to Egypt?" the emperor asked after a pause.

"I am sure, Caesar, it is," Tigellinus said.

The men looked at each other, smiling in silence.

"Why the hell does Albinus keep them from revolting," the emperor asked at last.

Both men burst with a Homeric laughter coming from the bottom of their hearts. In a minute, Tigellinus wiped tears from his eyes and said, "I remember Poppaea wanted to give a province to Gessimus."

"And you said, I need a province that I would not miss," the emperor said, and both men exploded with drunken laughter again.

* * *

The next morning, Tigellinus woke up in his house in a bad mood. Something worried him about the whole thing. Late last night, when he returned from the palace, a courier was waiting for him. He brought a few sheets of papyrus found by vigils in the cart of some Greek trader. The cart was confiscated a few months ago and nobody really looked inside. The papyrus contained detailed instructions for incendiaries and pointed directly to the Christians.

It seemed like a godsend, but something did not add up. Maybe I need to make some reality check, he decided, and sent for Benjamin. The lad knows a lot about his people, Tigellinus thought. He may know something about Christians as well, and anyway, he may be a good candidate to test the legend. He went to the garden in the back yard and sat in the chair in front of the pool. He rested his foot on the stone border of the pool, reclined in the chair, and got absorbed in his thoughts.

Benjamin came fast, with his hopes high and his desire to please the master even higher. This was the second time he got to talk to the master and his second chance to impress him and raise himself in the household. He stood in front of the master, waiting for his attention. Soon Tigellinus turned his eyes to him.

"What do you know about Christians?" Tigellinus asked.

"They are vile creatures, master," Benjamin said. "I think there is no crime that they would not do. I know a lot about them because I studied them."

"Studied?" Tigellinus asked.

"Yes, master," Benjamin said. "I'd like to write a book some day exposing their true intentions, showing them for what they are. I already have two chapters written. In these chapters I tell how they plan to burn Jerusalem."

"Really?" Tigellinus said. "How interesting. Why Jerusalem? Do you think they could try to burn Rome?"

"There is no crime they would not do," Benjamin said with a conviction. "Jerusalem is sacred for all Jews, and the Christian sect came from Judea, but I don't see why they could not try to hurt Rome either."

"I want to see these chapters," Tigellinus said. "Bring them at once."

Benjamin rushed out to bring his treasured manuscript. This clearly was his lucky day; the master not only talked to him, he asked for his manuscript. He just finished rewriting it based on his teacher's advice, and now he would show it to the master!

Tigellinus meanwhile took a cup of wine from the hands of a servant and continued to gaze at the shaky surface of the water pool. Could it be, he thought, that vigils were entertained by the fiction produced by his own slave?

In a few minutes Benjamin was back.

"Read," Tigellinus ordered without turning his head.

Benjamin started to read. A light smile was wondering on the prefect's face while he listened. No, he thought, it's clearly a completely different style. What a good lad. Such a naïve, "feel your vile joy." He chuckled. Who would speak about himself in such words? But the book may have some use. It would be a good way to prepare public opinion. He raised his hand, making a sign to stop reading.

"This is good," he said. "You are a smart kid, Benjamin, go ahead and write the book. I'll order that you will be given the time and material to write it. I want the book finished before September. By the way, where did you get the papyrus to write these chapters?"

"My teacher, ben Ata, gave it to me," Benjamin said. "He also advised me how to better put the words to describe the despicable abomination that those Christians are."

"Your teacher is a good man, Benjamin," Tigellinus said. The old dolt made the fake obvious, Tigellinus deduced, but anyway, in the end he gave some really good advice. Roman plebs are so stupid, that the book will work better the way it is now.

"On another matter," he continued. "Have you ever heard of the name Bin Jamen?"

"No, master," Benjamin said. "I've never heard of such a man."

"Who, do you think, he could be?"

"The name sounds like Nabatheans, master," Benjamin said. "That's the people of the Kingdom of Arabia."

"It sounds very much like your name," Tigellinus said.

115

"Yes, Nabathean people are related to us and they have somewhat similar names," Benjamin said. "But my name sounds somewhat different and it's a single word. It was the name of one of our patriarchs. No Jew would distort the name of one of our patriarchs."

"Good, good," Tigellinus said. So, nothing will point to Jews directly, he decided. That's good, the weapon must be directed precisely. When Christians are blamed, there should be no doubt that it's Christians, not somebody else. And a hint to Jews will not hurt either. Tigellinus chuckled – a province that you would not miss, truly so. He looked back to Benjamin, "Could this be the name of a Christian?"

"Why not, master? They accept all sorts of scum. There are Jews, Greeks, even Romans among them. Why should Nabatheans be an exception?"

"He is Christian," Tigellinus said. "Benjamin, you are a good boy, and I want to hear your opinion. Remember, what I tell you is secret. You should not tell it to anyone. People who cannot keep their mouths shut with these things don't live long. Do you understand?"

"I would never betray my master's trust," Benjamin said. He heard his heart beating in his ears. The master is going to entrust him with an important secret! That's the sure way up. Good bye, toilet cleaning!

"Good. Remember your words," Tigellinus said. "This Bin Jamen is really a Christian, he is the leader of some sect that's going to try to burn Rome on the third day of September Ides. That's why I need your book before September. I want to expose their crimes for the time when they will get their deserved penalty. By the way, here is how they really instruct their men to behave."

Tigellinus handed a piece of papyrus from the vigils quarters to Benjamin. He took it and started to read. As he progressed, his face went white and hands started to shake noticeably. What a good lad, Tigellinus thought, I even feel something like the voice of conscience about getting him into all this stuff. He considered it for a moment and then laughed mentally at himself. Conscience, duh! Meanwhile Benjamin finished reading and handed the papyrus back.

"You see?" Tigellinus said. "We know a lot about them. We even know the date and time they are going to strike. By the way, it's the third day of September Ides, right after sunset, put it into your book. And we know their leader's name – some Greek trader called Bin Jamen, as I already said. Mention this in the book too. And make them try to burn Rome, not Jerusalem, otherwise nobody will read it. Anyway, whether they succeed or not, they will be caught and executed. And I want Roman citizens to know their sins. It's your job to tell them."

"Thank you, master," Benjamin said with an eagerness while getting some of the color back to his face. "Thank you for your trust. I will not let you down!"

"I have no doubts about that," Tigellinus smiled. "Just remember, nobody should know what I've told you. You can talk with your teacher about that, it seems he gives you good advice. Warn him that if he wants to live to see the Christians punished, he should keep his mouth shut about it." The lad will certainly share this with his teacher anyway, he added mentally, so let him get the warning through.

Benjamin pressed his hands with papyrus to his heart showing with all his pose that he understood.

"Go," Tigellinus said and dismissively waved his hand.

* * *

The same day, Benjamin went to his teacher. They met again in the same study room.

"Let's start from how is your work and position in the house of the prefect going," ben Ata asked as usual.

Benjamin started to describe his meeting with the prefect and their conversation. As he got to more and more details, bet Ata looked more and more worried. He listened without interrupting, shaking his head occasionally, setting his hair straight, putting his hands to his temples like he had a headache. But he did not make a sign to stop, so Benjamin continued until he told everything.

Ben Ata thought for a while without saying anything, and Benjamin did not dare to ask the teacher what he thought about the whole thing.

117

"These are very dangerous things you've got yourself and me into," ben Ata said at last. "Very, very dangerous. By the way, when did the prefect say it's going to happen?"

"The third day of September Ides," Benjamin said. "Right after sunset."

"I wonder," ben Ata stroked his beard with a hand, "if the house of Doctor Noot will be affected," he paused for a moment looking over Benjamin's head. He thought for about a minute more. "Although, this could be a blessing. Seems like our Lord decided to get rid of this abomination that the Christians are. And He chose the Romans to be His tool, His sword in that. You may be blessed, Benjamin. You are going to turn this tool, the Romans, in the way our Lord wants them."

"But, teacher, what about my original manuscript? They think it's written by real Christians. What if they find that I am the author?" Benjamin stopped, realizing something terrible – he put his name there! He groaned and said, "Teacher, I've signed each piece of the original manuscript!"

"Trust the Lord, Benjamin," ben Ata said. "Do you know his plans? I don't. I just trust Him with all my heart and that's what you should do. Of course you signed it. Maybe that's how they've got the name of this Bin Jamen in the first place. You see, our Lord's plan already works. They have your manuscript, but they did not think about you. Why do you think it will change?"

"But if they do find out, they will throw me to the beasts."

"Trust the Lord, Benjamin," ben Ata repeated. "Even if they do throw you to the beasts, do you remember the story of prophet Daniel? He was thrown to the lions and they did not touch him. Nothing can happen against our Lord's will. Trust Him, and He will protect you. And you don't know if He will let you be thrown to the lions either. He already kept you safe, even while you were careless enough to lose the manuscript. You see, maybe this is a part of His plan. Who knows, maybe you will have to write more from the name of this Bin Jamen in the future? And even if not, you already gave Romans something to put the blame right."

"But what should I do, teacher?" Benjamin asked.

"Write the book just as your master instructed you," ben Ata said. "Keep your mouth shut. See what comes next. And, most importantly, trust the Lord."

"I will," Benjamin said. "Teacher, I did not understand one thing you said. What did you mean when you said that I may have to write more from the name of this Bin Jamin?"

"It seems to me that prefect got the name from your piece," ben Ata said. "It could happen that there is no Bin Jamen at all."

"But the master was so sure about it."

"Oh, he certainly has other information," ben Ata said. "But I wonder if this information has the name of the leader. It could be that your manuscript is the only place where they found the name. Think, what will happen if they do not find any 'Bin Jamen' around? They will not trust your manuscript. So you may have to write a few more pieces and make sure praetorians find them and bring them to the prefect."

"I see, teacher," Benjamin. "But is it not a false witness against the neighbor? And so many people will die. Is it not against 'Do not kill'?"

"No, but it's good that you think about that. Of course, we should follow the Commandments," ben Ata said with an approving smile. "But, Benjamin, what is following the Commandments if not obeying our Lord? You remember King Saul's war against Amalekites? Our Lord charged him to 'smite Amalek, and utterly destroy all that they have, and spare them not'. And so he did. But when King Saul left alive their King Agag, prophet Samuel came in anger and killed this last Amalekite with the sword by hewing him in pieces. Because it is said, 'to obey is better than sacrifice.' And the Book also says, 'for rebellion, is as sin of witchcraft, and stubbornness is as iniquity and idolatry.' Obey the Lord, Benjamin."

"I see," Benjamin said. "But how do I know, if the Lord wants me to do that."

"Trust the Lord, Benjamin," ben Ata said. "He'll find a way to tell you."

I GUESS NOT, YOUR HONOR
Chapter XVII, where Nil meets a not-very-good-Christian in the land that does not care about Rome

Several days passed after the conversation with the elderly priest of Amon-Ra. Nil, Galen, and Simaat talked to a lot more people with the same result. Nobody heard of a Christian named Benjamin trying to burn Rome, nobody was approached for help in such a venture, and nobody seemed to be involved either, at least when approached by three investigators. A few looked concerned, amused, or interested, but only as potential spectators rather than participants. In other words, there were no results unless one was willing to count a negative one as a result. Nil was not.

He visited the prefect once more, reported the status of the investigation, and asked for permission to leave for Heliopolis. The prefect was briefed daily by Galen on the findings, so he was not surprised, although visibly disappointed with the results. He supplied Nil with one more official paper requiring everybody to assist him in the investigation, and ordered Simaat to accompany Nil on the mission and help him get in touch with the local priests in Heliopolis.

The next day Nil and Simaat left the city. They boarded the river ship in the third internal harbor of Alexandria on Lake Mareotis. The harbor was located on the side of the city opposite the sea and provided the natural endpoint for river ships delivering grain and other merchandise from internal areas of the land. The ship had just brought a load of grain from Thebes, and now the captain was trying to get back before the river started to rise, converting a lot of dry land into shallow water almost indistinguishable from the fairway and very inconvenient. The ship was practically empty and the captain did not mind taking two passengers to Heliopolis. Not that he had much choice unless he was willing to incur the displeasure of both the Roman authorities and the Egyptian priesthood.

Galen had to stay in Alexandria to take care of some other important business on a personal assignment from the prefect, so

Nil and Simaat went alone. It's probably for the best, Nil decided. The presumptuous and rude Greek was ok to share a few bottles of wine with in a tavern accompanied by a few salty stories as a prologue to more entertainment, but working with him for days was not a pleasant experience at all. It was hard to say what the always dispassionate Simaat thought about that, but from the few hints, Nil suspected that the Egyptian shared the sentiment about their Greek colleague.

The ship was almost as large as Jason's *Tehe*. It was made of a wooden framework covered with wisps of papyrus reeds lashed together with rope. Despite the fragile material, the hull was watertight and felt sturdy enough to rely on. The crew consisted of the captain, who was also the owner of the vessel, four locals, and a legionnaire from the Theban garrison. The legionnaire was appointed to the ship to look that the grain was not stolen or replaced with a poorer grade on the way to Alexandria and now, mission accomplished, he was on the way back together with the rest of the crew.

The ship moved with two small sails up the river, the wind was neither strong, nor steady, and it took almost two days of unhurried voyage to reach Heliopolis. Most of the time vast marshlands covered the banks of the great river as far as one could see. The reed stood high, hiding fowl, crocodiles, deadly snakes, and an occasional hippopotamus family.

"Before the Romans and before the Greeks," Simaat said early in the first day, looking overboard, "this marshland was full of life, with an abundance of animals to hunt for."

"It does not look lifeless now either," Nil said.

"No, it does not," Simaat agreed. "We still supply some exotic animals for Roman arenas. But it's just a pale image of what was here before."

At twilight, the wind died out and a viscous silence covered the ship and the land around, accentuated only with frogs croaking and the occasional scream of a bird caught in its nest by an early night predator. Crocodiles, hunting in the darkness by their sense of warmth, were noiseless with only a rare splash of water so subdued that one would think that it's not real, but only seems to sound. A huge alien-looking moon was hanging low over the horizon, enlarged by the lens of moist air covering the marshlands of the Nile Delta. After the sun set, only this bizarre moon was giving its ghostly light to the unreal, motionless world that now surrounded the ship.

"I don't think we will find your incendiaries in Heliopolis either," Simaat said, looking at the picture around. The words sounded muffled in the air saturated with moisture.

Nil nodded. The whole world around was saying clear and loud, "I don't care." It existed long before Rome and it, probably, would still exist long after Rome becomes history. This world did not care for the little problems of the little people across the great sea who imagined themselves to be something of importance to the whole universe. Looking around, it was hard to believe in the very existence of Rome. It was like Nil was transferred to some other world where he could turn back, cross the sea, get to the seven hills and find them covered with the original forest without any trace of magnificent buildings and noisy crowds.

Nil shook himself. Maybe this world does not care, he said to himself, but I do. He wrapped himself up with the cloak and laid down to sleep. When he opened his eyes the next time, the wind blew again, and the ship was moving forward. On the stern the helmsman was working hard with the steering oar, keeping the ship on the fairway that was now clearly seen in the bright light of the high moon, still larger than normal but not frightening anymore.

At the end of the second day, they saw the golden apex of the benben stone, the central part of the Temple of Re located on the artificial mound in the center of the ancient city. The ship had to make a little detour to get to Heliopolis, as the city was not directly on the way from Alexandria to Thebes. It was located about five miles eastward from the apex of the Nile's delta, connected to the river with a channel. When the city was found, nobody was able to build it on the swamps that surrounded the river closely. A few centuries later, Egyptians partially diverted Nile's stream to build Memphis, but that was centuries later, so visitors to On, a.k.a. Heliopolis, had to travel a few extra miles to reach the city. The captain and his crew did not mind that at all. First, they did not have much of a choice, and more importantly, they were actually looking forward to the night in the house of beer justified by the state-ordered journey.

Landing sites in the city were quite simple. Most sites consisted of a city square surrounded by buildings from three sides and open to the channel on the fourth with small poles driven into the ground to rope boats. There were a lot of such sites because the river boats were occasionally used for moving around the city, although not all of them were functional now. The place was far past its former glory. Rectangular one- and two-story buildings with flat roofs were hiding their insides, but other signs betrayed abandoned sites.

The ship passed such a place. Undisturbed reeds hid the landing site. The square visible behind them was covered with grass with an occasional broken pot or amphora and a rotten two-wheel cart forgotten near one of the buildings that surrounded the square. The walls were covered with spots where the plaster fell off, revealing gray mudbricks – the primary construction material of the city. In one place, the mudbricks were worn by time and the weather to the point that the upper half of the wall collapsed. The breach revealed an empty second floor room with a wide bench made out of the same mudbricks going along the walls, and a single wooden pole in the middle supporting the ceiling. There was no human sounds around, no women chatting, no kids shouting, no footsteps, no squeaking wheels, only nature's own sounds disturbed the creepy silence of the place.

"There were two Persian invasions that almost destroyed this city during the last millennium," Simaat said pointing to the site. "The city never recovered after that. The parts around the temples are alive, but the farther ends of the city are all like that now."

"Who knows, it still may change," Nil said. "Now that our legions will not let enemies come here–"

"Your legions continue the work of Persians," Simaat interrupted him with a gloomy glance.

"How so?" Nil asked, puzzled by the change in the usually emotionless Egyptian.

"Did you see two *steles* in front of the royal palace in Alexandria?" Simaat asked. "You call them 'Cleopatra Needles', but neither of the queens named Cleopatra had anything to do with them. These steles were moved by the order of your Emperor Augustus to Alexandria from here, from the Temple of Ra in On. Ancestors of your Jewish wards saw them here on the dawn of their own history more than a millennium ago, when making the bricks for these buildings." He waved his hand to the house with the collapsed wall.

The view was not cheerful, and the conversation died. Soon they came close enough to the Temple, and the populated areas of the city started. They landed on a cobblestone city square facing the channel. Street traders were sitting on the ground near the walls under the sheds, with their merchandise spread out on the ground and hanging on the shed's poles in reed baskets.

Nil and Simaat said good bye to the crew and the captain, who already found that the nearest house of beer was right around the corner, and went to the city looking for an inn to stay in. After that the investigators went separate ways, Simaat left to arrange meetings with local priests for tomorrow, and Nil paid a visit to the local head of administration – *strategos*, the elderly Greek handling local affairs for Rome with his staff, consisting mostly of scribes.

Nil did not have to report here. With his credentials he could probably make the local strategos roll and bark, if he wanted to, but the old bureaucrat controlled the stream of information going from the nom to the province. He could have some information on Benjamin and his contacts, if the latter ever appeared in this city at all. And, yes, he had. Or, to be precise, the royal scribe and accountant had the information. Both were Egyptians in their early forties, with shaved heads, both wearing a traditional Egyptian kilt and a piece of white fabric covering their backs and the upper part of the arms. The latter was supposed to signify their status, as lower rank Egyptian men usually did not cover their upper body at all. Both were very proud of their status and eager to help the official from Rome with whatever they could. And they both spoke Greek pretty well. Here their similarity stopped. The scribe was scrawny, cold and acrimonious. In contrast, the accountant was stout and cheerful. Still, they were on good terms with each other and both knew their jobs very well.

"I need information on a man named Benjamin," Nil said. "We believe he is a Christian and a trader, he travels quite a bit, and that's pretty much all we know."

Both Egyptians listened attentively, trying to recollect any appropriate memory.

"We have about half a hundred Benjamins around," the accountant said. "Benjamin is a Jewish name, we have some Jews here, actually a lot of them. They even built a temple here about a century ago, and they still use it. Anyway, I believe only a few of them are Christians. We don't have their exact record, as they are all Jews for us, but comparing their number from tax records and the list from the temple, and assuming the missing ones are Christians, I'd say it should be less than a dozen."

"Rather about five or six, I'd say," the scribe corrected him with a rasping voice. "But none of them travel far enough and none of them are traders."

"What about ben Shlomo? I think his real name is Benjamin, son of Shlomo, right?" the accountant asked. "I think he may be a Christian."

"You are right, that's his real first name," the scribe agreed. "He is not on the synagogue list and he travels as far as Nubia and Rome."

"Tell me more," Nil said. "And where can I find him?"

"He is trading incense," the accountant said. "He buys them in upper Egypt, Red Sea Coast and Arabia and sells in Alexandria and Rome. He is pretty rich for modern days. You know, these are not the best times for Heliopolis. You'll find his house a few blocks to the sunset from the Jewish temple. Every street boy knows his house, it's easy to find."

"Thanks," Nil said. "I'll check him out. What about visitors to the city? I think the Benjamin that I look for is from Judea or Crete. Don't rely on that, but that's what I suspect. Do you remember any traders named Benjamin coming to the city lately?"

Both Egyptians thought for a bit, then the accountant shook his head.

"We have customs collection records," the scribe suggested. "Every trader coming to the city declares his merchandise and pays customs, if necessary. We can look there."

"Good idea," the accountant agreed. "I don't remember any Benjamin coming to the city, but the records may have one. Not that we have many traders coming here these years."

125

"Don't look too far back," Nil said. "If he came to the city, it was just a few months ago, this year for sure. How soon can you check the records?"

"Tomorrow by noon," the scribe said. "My records are in good order. It will not take too long."

"Thanks to you, both," Nil said. "I'll mention your help to the prefect in Alexandria. I'll be back after noon tomorrow then. Meanwhile, I'll check on this local trader of yours."

He gave a short salute to the men, turned away and left the building. When he got back to the inn, Simaat was already waiting for him. He had scheduled a meeting with the Great Seer, the high priest of the city, for tomorrow morning, where he could describe the problem and arrange for Nil to meet the high priest as well. Frankly, Nil was not sure why the meeting should be so complicated to arrange. If Nil had a mere *centuria* of soldiers behind him, he would go directly to this high priest, opening the doors with his foot, and talk to whoever he pleased to talk to. However, being alone, he was ok with following the local customs, especially if somebody else took care of all the formalities. He had a trader Benjamin to visit tomorrow morning, and it looked like the closest shot he had got so far.

* * *

The accountant was right: ben Shlomo's house was very easy to find. Nil gave a lepton – small copper Greek coin – to the boy who led him to the house, not that he had to, just for good luck, and knocked on the wooden door in the eight feet tall plastered mudbrick wall surrounding the yard and the house. Nobody seemed to care. Nil pounded the door with his fist several times, making enough noise to wake up all the famous Egyptian mummies within a mile radius and make them rush out to open the door. Still the silence was the answer. Nil started to think about breaking the door down, when a squeaking sound of poorly oiled hinges came from the depth of the yard and shuffling footsteps began to close on him.

"Who is there?" a rasping voice asked from behind the door.

"Centurion Nil Septimus of the first Praetorian Cohort wants to talk to your master," Nil said. "Open the door and get me to him."

A little window opened in the door revealing frightened eyes surrounded with wrinkles. The eyes surveyed the street and became even more frightened – Nil wore the full uniform and did not appear friendly. Looking at the wrinkles, it could really be a mummy woken up from some grave, Nil thought with a mental chuckle. Technically, what he said was not the complete truth. He was a centurion of the first *special* cohort of which the owner of the eyes never heard of in his life. But even if he had, Nil's objective was not to scare him to death literally, so it did not make any sense to go into such details. Anyway, the door opened and a very frightened old man in a Greek tunic and simple soleae sandals showed him the way to the house.

Nil was left in the small enclosed internal garden in front of the main entrance with a promise that the master of the house would show up shortly. A garden, pfff, rather a yard! Nil thought with a caustic smile. Four trees including a palm in the middle! He sat in the chair, brought by the servant, and looked around. Although, keeping these trees watered all the time could be a challenge in this climate, Nil admitted. He looked at the entrance to the house. Why receive me in the garden, he wondered. Nah, his house looks like a rathole. The morning air is fresh and cool, the sun does not burn yet. I am better off here. Interesting, most Egyptian houses look to me like ratholes, especially those deserted ones on the streets. I wonder why...

These thoughts kept him occupied for about ten minutes until the owner of the house showed up. Ben Shlomo, Benjamin, son of Shlomo, was a fat, short man about fifty years old with a bald spot on top of his head surrounded by sparse, curly and mostly gray hair. He wore a white Greek chlamys on top of a simple off-white tunic, and got to the guest barefooted, apparently in a hurry. His chubby face, with full lips, wide nose and round cheeks, was speaking for itself.

"What can I do for you?" ben Shlomo asked with an obsequious smile.

That's not him, Nil decided. This pot-bellied guy could be a cheater, pilferer, adulterer, but definitely not a rebel. Oh, well, I did not expect *that* Benjamin to reside in this city anyway. Just doing due diligence. If I wasted my morning on him, let me at least question him on the local Christian community and any other traders who could have visited the city. This guy seemed to be a cooperative type.

"Ben Shlomo?" Nil asked.

The trader readily nodded. "Yes, that's me, Your Honor."

"Strategos of the city recommended you as a trustworthy and a decent man who can help me with my business," Nil said. "You are a Christian, right?"

"Well, you can say that, I guess," ben Shlomo said.

Nil frowned. "What do you mean? Do you go into the Christian community as one of their own?"

"Yes, Your Honor, I do," ben Shlomo nodded again without stopping to smile.

"That's all I need," Nil said. "So tell me a few things about the local Christians. Do they tell a lot of those stories about the end of the world, Rome being destroyed, you know how it goes, right?"

"Well, Your Honor," ben Shlomo said without a smile but still with a servile expression on his face. "They are very poor people living a very hard life. I guess the end of the world promises a lot of hope to them. That's why they need all these tales."

"You don't believe these tales, do you?" Nil asked.

"Oh, no," ben Shlomo chuckled and a smart, skeptical man showed up for a moment from behind the obedient mask. "No, Your Honor, of course, I don't. Why would I try to continue to make money, if I thought the world would end tomorrow?"

"Then why did you join the Christians?" Nil asked.

"Well, Your Honor, first of all, the Jews here go to the local temple, and some people are questioning, is it a right thing to have a second temple?" ben Shlomo said. "Besides, the priests in the local temple are really strict about tithing. And, you know, it's not a good time for business here in Heliopolis; I don't make as much money as they expect me to. People are asking what ben Shlomo is doing in this city anyway, maybe he should move to Alexandria. And I don't disagree with them. It's just very expensive to go to the local temple here. As to these people, I mean Christians, they are so poor, they are happy with whatever I can share out of the kindness of my heart. Besides, it's good for the business. If you say you are a Christian, nobody expects you to cheat them."

"You are not a very good Christian, are you?" Nil chuckled.

"I guess not, Your Honor," ben Shlomo said and shook his head. "Poor ben Shlomo is so busy with the trade, it takes a lot of time to make the money. And if somebody asks if I should become good at faith, or should I make money to feed those poor people, I'd say make the money. I guess, you are right, Your honor. Poor ben Shlomo is not a very good Christian."

"I thought so," Nil said. "Anyway, getting back to the business. So they like the tales. Is there anybody who'd like to make them happen faster? Say, by revolting or doing harm to Rome?"

"No, I don't think so," ben Shlomo said. "They wouldn't do anything like this. Harm Rome? How would they get there in the first place? Many of them are not rich enough to pay the fare to Alexandria."

"And would you?" Nil asked. "Would you like to see something happen to Rome?"

"Why would I?" ben Shlomo said. "I would not pretend that I love Rome, there is nothing there to me personally. But for my business, oh, no. That would be terrible. When something wrong happens, people stop buying incense, they buy food instead. That would ruin me!"

Definitely not him, Nil thought again. He'd probably inform authorities on his own if he hears anything. But let's ask anyway.

"Fine, let's leave this alone," Nil said. "On another matter. Have you ever met a Christian trader named Benjamin?"

"My name is Benjamin, Your Honor," ben Shlomo said.

"I know," Nil said, "I want to know if you ever met some other trader named Benjamin?"

"Not many," ben Shlomo said. "Once, two years ago, I met one on Crete, and he was Christian, all right. We spent a night in a tavern there, and then went different ways. I was going to Rome and he was returning to Judea."

"Did he speak about any stuff that's going to happen to Rome?"

"Sure, he did, Your Honor," ben Shlomo said. "All Christians are really fond of these tales. I wonder why he was, he was not poor, but he paid for food and wine, and I listened to whatever he wanted to say."

That could be him, Nil thought. Clearly, it was before he started with his plans, it was two years ago. That's why he did not mention the plans. But this could be him.

"Tell me, what did he look like?" Nil asked.

"Well, he had a beard and moustache, Your Honor," ben Shlomo started. "He did not have a bald spot like me. He was much younger, thirty, maybe forty or so. You know, this age when men get crazy ideas, maybe a little older than that. He was taller than me, and he looked really strong and healthy."

"Anything special?" Nil asked. "Birthmarks, scars, some funny way he speaks or walks?"

"No, Your Honor," ben Shlomo shook his head. "Nothing like that, just a man like many others around."

"Did he mention where he lives?" Nil asked.

"He was going to Joppa," ben Shlomo said. "But I believe he has a house in Jerusalem. Among other things, he also trades spices and incense from Arabia. Jerusalem is practically on the way there. He gave me some good hints on selling my merchandise in Rome. I visited Rome twice since then and each time the buyer that he referred me to gave me a good profitable price."

"Thanks, that's all I need to know for now," Nil said. "So, you say you are not a very good Christian, huh?"

"I guess not, Your Honor," ben Shlomo shrugged his shoulders.

IT BECOMES A HABIT
Chapter XVIII, where Nil sees a black cat in a dark room

Nil and Simaat met in the inn around noon. The Egyptian talked to the High Priest and brought good news – the Great Seer, which was the official title of the High Priest, would see Nil tomorrow after the sun set. They spent the rest of the day and most of the next day visiting smaller local temples and talking with their priests. The result was about the same as in Alexandria. The priests had no clue, nor any interest in the whole affair. They obediently promised to look for Benjamin, three of them even pointed to ben Shlomo as a possible suspect, but that was as far as it went.

Simaat led Nil to the Temple of Ra right after the sun set. The moon was not up yet, so Nil did not see much on the way in. The humid warm air of the night was filled with the sounds of the city preparing for the night rest. The cry of an infant, the excited shouting of kids playing in a house, the conversation of a lucky family who could afford having the late night meal – all these sounds were coming from the two-story buildings surrounding the street, with their windows highlighted with the light-orange light of oil lamps. Some of the windows were not covered with anything and, passing, Nil could see what was happening inside: a woman sitting with her back to the window, nursing the baby; two old men playing some board game on the floor; a younger, probably, married couple enjoying the company of each other. Well, Nil thought, these two are going to cover their window soon, certainly before going to the floor. As Nil and Simaat came closer to the Temple, multi-story, multi-family dwellings were slowly replaced with one-floor houses hiding behind the walls in the depth of large yards and, sometimes, gardens. Human sounds became rarer, muffled while crossing yards and walls.

The Temple appeared suddenly in front of them. Cobblestone pavement changed to flat limestone slabs under their feet. They passed the alley of sphinxes and came to the gates in a high wall that towered above them like a huge dark mass. The priest at the gate was expecting visitors. He took a torch and led both Nil and Simaat into the first court.

"The Great Seer said that you will wait here," the priest told Simaat, then turned to Nil. "Follow me. The Great Seer is in the library."

They crossed the yard, passed the main entrance in the middle, and entered the arc in the right wall of the court. The yard behind was much smaller, with exits on the right and on the left, and a building with colonnade in the far end. As they came closer, Nil noticed that the flower-shaped columns were yellow for most of their length, except the buds on the top painted as bright flowers, although in the unsteady yellow light of a torch it was hard to say what colors were used. They went through the front door and entered a hall about fifty feet wide and a hundred feet long lightened with multiple oil lamps on high stands. Benches went along the walls with embedded shelves and lockers. The hall was empty except for a single man in the far left corner and a few cats. The Great Seer walked to Nil, and dismissed the priest with the sign of his hand.

"Speak," he said to Nil in Greek after the priest left the hall.

The High Priest turned and started to walk slowly, so that Nil had to follow him while explaining the whole story again. The Great Seer was old, maybe seventy years old or more, with a strong lean body and a cleanly shaved head. He wore a Greek chlamys on top of white Egyptian kilt going below his knees. His clear and thoughtful eyes were looking aside like he is not listening. He picked up a black kitten from the floor, put it on one hand, and started to pet the little furball with another. The kitty seized the opportunity, grasped the priest's hand with all four clawed paws and enthusiastically started to bite the edge of his palm with its little sharp teeth. The palm was almost as wide as the kitty's mouth so it took a bit until it could really achieve its goal. Then, as if afraid that it would take even more time to repeat it, the kitty stopped with an almost meditative expression in its eyes, its paws around the priest's arm and its mouth wide open and busy with the edge of the priest's palm. The priest did not react to all these involutions and continued to pet the little beast. He stopped in front of a bronze polished mirror standing on the bench.

"Watch," he said and put the kitten in front of the mirror. The kitty fixed its eyes on its own reflection and arched its back with its hair standing on end and its pointing-up- tail three times thicker than usual. Then it raised a paw and hissed loudly without ever moving its eyes. The priest picked it up from the bench, put back on his left hand and started to pet him again. The little feline relaxed and began to purr.

"Cats are noble animals," the priest said with affection and smiled. "This one is just very young."

Nil did not answer, waiting for an explanation. The priest let the kitty go to the floor and turned. His confident, clean and calm eyes were now fixed on Nil.

"We are not young, Roman," he said. "We don't fight with our own reflections."

They stood for a moment in the unsteady light of the oil lamps in front of each other – an old priest with vivid thoughtful eyes and a young, strong, confused man in Roman uniform. Then Nil broke the silence.

"I understand this means that I will not find my answers here," he said.

"It means that you will not find your arsonists here," the priest said softly. "The answers – I don't know – most people carry their answers with themselves, they just don't like them."

"But who else can carry out such a plan, if not you?" Nil asked.

"Everybody," the priest said simply. "You don't need wisdom to do things. You need some to know how to do things, but even that is just knowledge, not wisdom."

"But how can a mere man set fire to a huge city without the gods' help?" Nil asked. "It's impossible, isn't it?"

"Gods," the priest laughed softly. "What's your name, young man?"

"Nil Septimus, didn't Simaat tell you?"

"Nil," the priest said thoughtfully, ignoring the question. "It's a powerful name. Well, I have tomorrow night free, why not spend it talking to you. Come here an hour before sunset and bring your questions."

"Why not tonight?"

"Because tonight I am busy, Roman," the priest said with a calm smile. "Tonight I am talking to stars about you."

Nil met astrologers before. Some of them were plain liars. They could not read stars, and nothing they promised happened or happened as expected. Others were more knowledgeable, giving a hope that this particular man could see the future. The words of the Great Seer felt different. The priest did not promise anything, he simply mentioned it as a matter of fact. In the same way Nil would say that he would be busy sharing a bottle of wine with an old friend. Consciously skeptical, Nil rarely, if ever, trusted astrologers, but deep inside Nil felt that this was exactly what was going to happen tonight, that the old man would somehow talk to the stars, not merely read them. Even more, he felt that the stars would care to talk back. The priest clapped his hands and a junior priest showed up from outside.

"Tomorrow, an hour before sunset," the Great Seer said.

Nil saluted, turned, and went outside after the guide. On the way to the exit he solemnly shook his head. The delusion did not want to go. Oh well, Nil decided at last, it does not matter where the help comes from. If this Egyptian can consult the stars and they say something useful, so much the better.

On the way back to the inn Nil asked Simaat, "Do you think he will really talk to the stars about me?"

"If he said," the Egyptian answered, "he will."

"Still, I don't get it," Nil said. "Why did he refuse to talk today?"

"The time flows differently here," Simaat said.

"What do you mean?"

Simaat stopped in the middle of the dark street. The torch light highlighted his face and his right hand.

"If your people are as old as the pyramids, Roman," he said, "you start to think before speaking or acting. If your people built the pyramids, it becomes a habit."

"And if you are younger than the pyramids?" Nil asked, slightly annoyed with Simaat's words.

"This question you should bring to the Great Seer tomorrow," the Egyptian said.

OH, SHIT!
Chapter XIX, where Nil hears a lot of things he finds hard to believe

In the daylight the Temple looked even more impressive than in the night. The high walls, made of yellowish, almost white, limestone, were interrupted with the massive towers of the gate. In the first court a junior priest told Nil to wash his hands and face in a large stone bowl on a high stand, and his feet in a special basin built into the court's pavement. Then, still barefooted, they proceeded straight ahead into the main internal gates.

The priest led Nil and Simaat into a wide covered passageway going up from the valley into the Upper Temple built on an artificial mound dominating the city. There were no windows in the walls so only the oil lamps were giving a murky light to the way. Dark niches and alcoves were opening on the right and on the left, but it was hard to see whether they were occupied with anything or were empty. The strong smell of incense was filling the air.

"It's a great honor, Roman," Simaat said quietly. "You will be allowed to attend the service. Wait until it ends, and the Great Seer may be inclined to tell you much more than you would get otherwise."

Nil just nodded back. He had already come to the same conclusion, and was ready to waste an hour watching the ceremony. Egyptian priests were famous for their closeness and for keeping their secrets. A little leverage like that would certainly be beneficial, Nil decided, if not now, sometime later. Still, there was an uncomfortable feeling. How did this ceremony go and what is his role in it, Nil wondered and some second thoughts popped up in his mind.

"I hope I will be able to hear what he says afterward," Nil asked Simaat quietly.

"No matter what you've heard, Roman, we don't sacrifice humans," Simaat answered giving Nil a haughty glance. "We don't even sacrifice bulls."

Nil looked at him, trying to figure if he could trust these words.

"Anyway, you left your sandals at the entrance, not your sword," Simaat shrugged his shoulders. "What are you afraid of?"

He is right, Nil decided, none of Egyptians had a weapon on them and, anyway, it was unlikely they would risk harming a Roman official.

The light at the end of the passageway grew larger and larger until they entered the internal court of the Upper Temple. Evening light flooded the place and looked especially bright after the darkness of the passageway. A rectangular base, about ten feet tall, with doors in it, occupied the center of the yard. A gold-plated pyramid-shaped benben stone was shining bright in the light of the setting sun on top of the high pedestal. The pedestal was in the shape of a narrow truncated pyramid or a very wide – many paces in diameter – stele located on the top of the base.

The High Priest was standing at the altar in front of the pedestal facing the sun. His hands were raised high and he was chanting something loudly in Egyptian. The junior priest led Nil to a group of priests standing in the yard, watching the High Priest and the sun, mostly silent, occasionally repeating separate words of the Great Seer. Nil stood behind them, observing the ceremony.

The sun was setting. Soon the shadows covered the yard, the priest, the basement, and started to climb the pedestal. Up, up, and now only the golden benben stone was shining from above. The chanting become louder, and all the other priests joined the Great Seer in the prayer. They probably wish a victory to their god, Nil thought unable to understand the words of the alien language. While investigating in Alexandria and here, in Heliopolis, Nil heard some Egyptian legends including one about the Sun-god fighting the evil snake to ensure that the next day comes.

Anyway, the last ray of sun went out, the chanting stopped, and the crowd of priests dispersed, each of them busy with other affairs. The High Priest turned to them. He was dressed for the ceremony in simple sandals, a blue kilt embroidered with white, yellow and red multi-cornered stars; a belt with multi-colored gems going around his waist; wide flat collar around his neck made of white, red and blue gems and covering his shoulders and uppermost part of his breast and back; and a striped white and red headcloth covering his shaved head.

"You can go now. Wait in the inn," he said to Simaat, and dismissed the guide with a simple gesture. After they left, he turned to Nil.

"Let's take a walk on the wall," he said and pointed to a narrow stairway going up on the side of the Temple wall to the very top. On the way he said something in Egyptian to a junior priest passing by, who went off and brought a lighted torch in less than a minute.

"He does not speak Latin or Greek, so we can talk freely," the Great Seer said and started to climb the stairs. Nil and the junior priest followed.

The wall on the top was about fifty feet wide. It was wider than many of the streets of Heliopolis, which laid outside of the walls in the soft light of the dusk. The priest leaned his elbow on a stone parapet looking over the city into the river and the surrounding marshlands.

"So, tell me, why did you come here to find your criminals?" he asked.

"I thought that you were the only people who could really do such a thing," Nil said. "Burning a huge city without taking it over – I don't know anybody else who can do that."

"In other words, you thought that you knew something about this land, and based on that, you decided that we are the only ones who can do that, right?"

"Yes, that's what I said," Nil agreed.

"Actually, you are wrong on both accounts," the priest said.

"Both?"

"Yes, anybody can burn Rome and you don't know anything about this land."

"Yes, you already told me so yesterday," Nil said. "Only I have trouble believing you. How can anybody do that?"

"Easily," the priest said. "Take twenty people you trust. You are centurion, right? That's one fifth of your people. Dress them as traders from different provinces and lands. Send them to

Rome different ways, apart from each other. When in Rome, they should rent a dwelling in the same district. Choose the district with the most crumbled space and more wooden houses. Then, on a fixed day at a fixed time each of them must spill some oil around their rooms, start the fire, and quietly leave. When the fire grabs many houses, let them run on the streets and cry that they lost their houses, or just make them leave Rome at once. Twenty fires started in the same district will make it impossible for vigils to put them all out. When the whole district is on fire, nobody will be able to stop it from spreading to the other districts. Can you do anything against such a plan?"

So simple, Nil thought, and so efficient. So deadly efficient. I was right, only these people could do that.

"Notice," the priest said, like he was hearing Nil's thoughts, "that almost anybody can do it. You don't need an Egyptian for that. Greek, Jew, Roman – does not matter. In fact, you can do it."

"Then why did nobody think of it before?" Nil asked. "Rome has plenty of enemies. Parthians would pay gold for such a plan."

"Because," the priest said slowly and clearly, "most people don't think at all."

"I think," Nil said.

"Did you think of this plan?"

"No."

"Most people don't think," the priest repeated. "When you think, you have a purpose, you ask the right questions, and you get the right answers. What most of the people do is not thinking, it's daydreaming. What's happening in their minds has no clear purpose, they ask wrong questions, and they get wrong answers, sometimes not even related to the wrong questions they just asked themselves."

"Then we get back to the Egyptians, right?" Nil asked. "You say that people don't think, and you need to know how to do something before you actually do it, right? Who else?"

"Thank you for your faith in my people," the priest said with an ironic tone. "However, we are not the only people capable of thinking. Some Greeks think," the priest paused, then added, "occasionally. And some Romans are not hopeless either. When

Plato studied with one of my predecessors, it was not so bad. Not a star student, of course, but not bad at all."

"Then who may think of that, to help the Christians?" Nil asked.

"Why do you think that Christians are involved at all?"

"They hate Rome and they prophesy its destruction, right?" Nil said.

"That's bullshit, young man," the priest said. "Religious fanatics may want to do something, but they are rarely capable of really doing it. Their minds are blurred with an artificial world they create for themselves."

"'Bullshit'?" Nil smiled. "I thought, bulls are holy here in Egypt."

"That's another bullshit, young man," the priest said indifferently. "But let's talk about it later. You see, your problem is that you are doing it the wrong way. Remember, purpose-question-answer. You are trying to start with an answer, which is a completely top down way. Do you know what your purpose is?"

"To prevent the fire from happening, I assume; to save Rome," Nil said.

"So, to prevent or to save? These are different purposes," the priest said.

"To save," Nil said after a momentarily delay.

"Good," the priest said thoughtfully and paused. "You are worth spending some time on. Anyway, tell me, if your purpose is to save Rome, why do you care about the fire?"

"Isn't that what threatens Rome?" Nil asked. "Besides, that's what my current assignment is."

"No, it's not what threatens Rome," the priest said. "You Romans own the world, you will rebuild Rome even better than it is now. The empire will only get stronger after that. A fire cannot do much harm to Rome itself. And I have some second thoughts about your assignment as well."

"But it will harm Romans," Nil said. "Some will die in the fire, some will starve."

The priest crossed his arms on his chest, then propped up his chin with his left fist, looking at Nil, puzzled. "You may be really worth the effort."

"So, assuming we want to prevent the fire, what would be the right question?" Nil asked.

"You know the right question," the priest said. "You Romans made it a principle in your judicial system. *Qui bono?* Who profits? Imagine that the fire already happened. Dismiss religious fanatics, victims of unshared love, fools craving for great deeds. They may be involved, but they are all just pawns. At the heart of conspiracy are always people who want two things – power and money. In Rome it may actually be the other way around, though... but it does not matter. Power and money, money and power. Who will get more power and more money? They are the people you are looking for."

Nil stood dumbfounded and not knowing what to say.

"You are really worth the effort, Nil," the priest said with a smile. "A fool in your place would already start shouting that I am wrong. Shocked?"

"I should be," Nil said, slowly picking the words. "And I don't like what I've heard. But you are right. In fact, that's how I do most of my investigations."

"Good," the priest said and nodded. "Why not do that now?"

"If you are right, that means..." Nil said and looked at the priest.

"That means that your arsonists are in Rome," concluded the priest for Nil with a slight nod.

"Oh, shit!" It was the only thing Nil could say.

"I cannot agree more," the priest shrugged his shoulders, waiting for Nil to come to his senses. "That's why I had doubts about your assignment."

Nil recalled his meeting with the prefect. He said, "It's strange that the enemies can do such a great service for the Empire..." He also said, "For the real loyalty."

"Oh, shit!" Nil said again.

"You are repeating yourself," the priest noted.

Nil looked to the darkness outside – the dusk was almost already gone and the moon had not risen yet. They kept silent for a few minutes.

"Then I need to go back to Rome and make the prefect stop with this plan, right?" Nil said at last.

"You are starting with the answers again," the priest noticed dispassionately.

Nil looked back to the darkness behind the wall. You start to think before speaking or acting, Nil recalled Simaat's words from yesterday's conversation. Maybe that's what he needs to do. To think.

"So how can I prevent that?" Nil asked.

"That's a question," the priest said. "It's better than starting with an answer, but it's still a wrong way."

"How do I find the purpose?" Nil asked.

"That's a much better question," the priest said with a smile. "Most people never go so far. And we will talk about that today."

Nil turned again to the darkness outside.

"So, no gods, just men," he said at last.

"No gods," the priest agreed. "May I ask, what do you need gods for?"

"To help, to protect," Nil said. "Well, actually, you don't as much need gods, they just are."

"No, they are not," the priest said.

"You don't believe in gods?" Nil asked. "I would not expect that from an Egyptian."

"It's not about what I believe in," the priest said patiently. "It's about what exists and what does not. There are no gods. There is God, the one and the only."

"You sound like a Jew," Nil said.

"Oh, those exiles," the priest said.

"According to them, they put up quite a fight to get out," Nil said remembering his conversations with some Jews when he just started to investigate Christians.

"Of course they say that." The priest shrugged his shoulders. "If you need to know, it was a very long time ago. They were very odd people. Their holy people did not shave and did not wash their bodies much either. It was like a condition of holiness, can you imagine anything as stupid? Our priests shave their bodies and fast on water for several days before entering the holiest of holy of our temples. These people saw it differently. So the rest of them did not fancy shaving their heads either. And if you live in a hot swamp – that's where On is – and

141

don't shave, you are getting a lot of nasty stuff in your hair. Their quarter was an abomination to this city. Swarms of flies multiplied in the remains of animals that they used to slaughter and eat. Their sewage polluted the river and it was not safe to drink water down the stream from them. During one of their celebrations, the water became red with the blood of the stock they slaughtered, and the frogs were jumping out of the river, unable to live in such water. Then, naturally, they got some sickness, and it spread around the city. It was especially bad on children. We had to exile them."

He stood up, sighed, and started to pace slowly along the parapet. Nil and the priest with the torch followed him.

"I feel pity for them. Can you imagine leaving everything you have, being forced to go? People of On gave them some money, gold and gems for the road, to buy food on the way – you know, as any good neighbor would do – but I doubt it helped them much. Our priest from this temple, Osarsiph, promised to take them to a good place to live, where there is enough land and food for them and their animals. He left, leading them North and keeping their hopes up. They called him Moses. I understand he became their prophet. On the way he taught them how important it is to be clean, cleanness is the cornerstone of their beliefs now. He also taught them the same thing I just told you. There are no gods, there is only one true God. And after that, it looks like he really fulfilled his promise. I'd say they found their place now, and the whole thing was very good for them."

He paused.

"How do you know all of this?" Nil asked.

"We have some records from those times," the priest said. "Not much survived after the Persian invasions, but still we have some. And there are things that I heard from my predecessor and older priests when I was younger."

"Heard?"

"Yes, heard. When an older priest teaches an apprentice the geography and what's around, and they come to Judea, this is what the apprentice learns. And if you are asking me how reliable this information is, understand that it was very long ago, and Jews never were a special point of interest to us."

"I thought that of all people, you would know for sure," Nil said. "After all, you were around when it all happened."

"And you were around traveling here from Alexandria merely days ago," the priest said. "What if you sit down now and describe your way on a papyrus? Would it be reliable?"

"Yes," Nil said. "Unless I'd have a reason to lie."

"But nobody who reads it will know if you had such a reason or not. And that's not all. Say, who did you travel with?"

"Simaat, priest from Alexandria and the head of their temple police, a legionnaire from the Thebes garrison–" Nil started.

"No, you traveled with the second prophet of the Temple of Isis, also called the First Priest," the old man interrupted him. "You see, even when an author doesn't have any reasons to lie, you still don't know if he is telling the truth. That's what history is about, taking the knowledge a droplet after a droplet, carefully comparing it, trying to make sense. That's the only way you can hope to find the truth about the past. After all, you are an investigator, you should know that."

He paused again, continuing his slow pace.

"Anyway, it's not me talking like a Jew, it's them talking like us," the priest returned to the topic. "They took it all from here."

"They would disagree with you," Nil said.

"Of course, they will," the priest said. "Don't be stupid. Just watch and compare. I take it you never read their sacred texts?"

"I didn't," Nil admitted.

"Then ask them, when you have a chance, how many people came to Egypt and how many left it," the priest said. "And to save the time, I'll tell you what their own sacred texts tell. Here came less than a hundred people – a single family. They emerged from here as a people in the hundreds of thousands. So, where did they become a people, not a mere family?"

"I see your point," Nil said.

The priest parted his hands. "Do you want to hear more? Ask them about the Ark of the Covenant, as they call it. It's a box with handles which should be in the holiest of holy of their Temple. Similar arks are almost in every temple in this land; they are supposed to be the residence of their 'gods'. Of course, you will not find one in this temple, the true God cannot live in a box, that's ridiculous, but as a matter of fact, Jews copied it."

"They may say that you copied it."

"No offense to your friends, but that would be hard to believe," the priest said with a smile. "You see, they were here at the time that we call a 'New Kingdom'. 'New' stands here for a reason. We are a little older than that."

"'A little'? Then it could be true."

"What a naïve mind," the priest said and laughed shortly. "It's beautiful. Let me explain that. Romulus and Remus were saved by a wolf about seven or eight centuries ago. No offense, you Romans are quite good kids… very promising. It's just that you are really young. Jews built their first temple about ten or eleven centuries ago. Now about this land. We were here for about fifty centuries, and our first king ruled this land about thirty centuries ago."

The priest paused, looking at Nil. "Got the idea?"

"Yes," Nil said grasping the joke. "Your 'little' is rather large."

"Precisely. Another example," the priest said, "I take it you met their High Priest while you were in Jerusalem?"

"Yes, I did," Nil said.

"Did you notice a large square thing with multi-colored gems fixed to his breast?"

"Yes," Nil said. "I remember I wondered why he needs one."

"He does not," the priest said. "It's just a reflection, a memory. This belt," he pointed out to his belt with gems going around his waist, "was only permitted to the kings and High Priests. They made it larger and positioned it so that everybody could see it."

"But they have just one god," Nil said. "And Egyptians have a lot of temples to different ones."

"Temples, yes," the priest agreed. "Do you remember what was the temple, where a priest sent you to On?"

"Amon-Ra in Alexandria," Nil said.

"I take it, they don't worship Amon there in Jerusalem, right?" the priest asked.

"No, they recognize only one god."

"Now tell me, how do they end their prayers?" the priest asked. "Or how do Christians end their prayers, it's the same word, and you should have heard it many times."

"Amen?" Nil said.

"Amon, amen..." the priest twisted his palm one way then another in an uncertain gesture. "Anyway, as I said, Osarsiph taught them well and it serves them well to follow the main secret of this temple and be faithful to the true God."

"One and the only god is the main secret of this temple?" Nil asked. "Then why have you told me?"

"Because you've asked," the priest said. "I will not tell it to the crowd the way I told it to you, of course. You came the long way, you came to me and asked. You deserve to hear your answer."

"What if I start to tell everybody your secret?" Nil said.

"Go ahead," the priest shrugged his shoulders. "Who would believe you? Jews were doing that for a millennium, are there many people listening?"

"And what if I refer to you?"

"Had anybody ever heard me recognizing any god but the true and the only one?" the priest asked. "People listen, but they don't hear. You see, true temple secrets are guarded differently than little people secrets. Whoever should not know the secret, he just cannot comprehend it. That's it. Unless people are ready, you can preach in a wilderness as well."

"Your secrets are guarded well," Nil said, slowly trying to digest what he heard.

"They are," the priest agreed. "Isn't it sad?"

"You also seem to know a lot about Jews."

"Yes, I fancied them when I was an apprentice. I had an affair with a Jewish girl, so I looked for pieces of knowledge about her people. Seems like I collected a lot. In a sense, I am somewhat proud of them, at what they achieved. Jews may be pesky and annoying, but they are our people, they are part of us. They may even outlive this land. Who knows, in a time they could be the last people of Kemet around."

"I did not expect to hear anything like that from you, or from any Egyptian for that matter," Nil said, rubbing his cheek pensively.

"Of course you did not. You don't have a clue about what this land is," the priest said. "Tell me, what made you think that you would get your answers here in the first place?"

"Well, Egypt is old and mysterious, as well as the Nile that feeds you," Nil said. "You are different from the rest of us. Your gods help you, and Egyptian priests know how to talk to them. You possess many powers that nobody else has. Your kings were gods too—"

The priest raised his hand, and Nil stopped.

"The only correct thing you said, is that we are mysterious to you," the priest said. "Let see, first of all: the name of this land is not Egypt, it's Kemet, 'the Black Land'. 'Aegyptus' is the Greek word. They probably distorted something from our language but nobody, including them, can recognize what it was. Actually, Greeks gave up guessing and invented a myth about a king with such name that ruled this land. Completely fictional king, of course. We are still a mystery to them. Anyway, this land is called Kemet, 'The Black Land' as an opposed to 'the Red Land', the dry, hot and dead *Deshret* that surrounds Kemet. Kemet is the land of black soil that is made fruitful by *Iteru*, the River. 'Nile' is another Greek name, meaning 'river valley'. About powers – how do you think it happened that we are ruled by Rome? So much for the power. No offense, you, Romans, are good kids, but you just need the time to grow and learn."

"You are referring to Romans as kids the second time," Nil said. "Why?"

"Because you are kids," the priest said. "Our kids. Of our empire, of Kemet."

"I find it hard to believe, Egyptian," Nil said screwing up his eyes.

"It's not the first thing you found hard to believe today, is it?" the priest said. "You said that we revere our kings as gods. Does 'Divine Augustus' ring a bell? Did it strike you that Rome got it's first emperor after the future emperor married our queen and had a child from her?"

"But this child did not become an emperor!"

"Your loss," the priest noticed. He walked to the internal side of the wall and leveled a thin layer of sand on the parapet with his hand. "Draw me the first letter of your alphabet here," he said.

Nil draw the capital letter 'A' on the sand with his finger.

The priest nodded, and then waived his hand toward the obelisk with benben stone. "Looks familiar?"

Nil looked at the obelisk. Now, in the light of raising moon with only its silhouette visible, it was really similar to a very large and narrow letter 'A'.

The priest added a little circle on top of the letter, making it 'Å'. "You, probably, are more accustomed to seeing this symbol around here; it's just a variation, a pyramid, the benben stone meeting the first ray of rising Sun. Another interpretation is an eye on top of the pyramid meeting the first ray of the rising sun. Who knows what religious artifacts of the future will fancy it?"

He kept a silence for a moment.

"Want more? Your Roman eagle is our falcon Horus. Here is the purpur of your emperors," he said and pointed out to the red stripe on his headcloth. "And here, the white robes of your priests," he said pointing to a white stripe. "And only God knows how many future empires are here," he pointed to his kilt with three, four, five, and six-corner stars. "Kemet is a crib of the civilization, and the mother of civilizations. It's a light in the darkness, and we witnessed how this light gave reflections first, then sparks, and then the sparks became new lands and new people."

He took the torch from the junior priest and dismissed him. Then he walked to the outer side of the wall and raised the hand with the torch high. Orange glimpses reflected in the water of the channel down below.

"You see, even this minuscule light makes reflections in the river," the priest said. "And what if the light is really bright? You cannot be bright and have no reflections, no progeny."

He threw out the torch high up into the air. It threw a ball of sparks, reflected in the water like a silent fire, and then disappeared below in the darkness.

"It went off," Nil said.

"Yes, it did," the priest said. "And so will we some day. But not every spark is dead. One fell on the dry land of Judea. Another on the dry grass on Palatine Hill. Who knows where the others landed. I only can say that some time in the future the world will be full of our reflections, our children fighting each other like the 'gods', the children of Re of our legends."

"You seem very confident about all this," Nil said.

"Yes, I am," the priest answered. "It's actually very simple. You Romans can deny your heritage and continue to be young and stupid. Or you can be proud of it, and count your history for fifty centuries. It's your choice."

He turned to Nil, rested upon the parapet, almost sat on it, and crossed his arms on his breast.

"Look," Nil said, slowly picking the words. "You may be right, but what I cannot accept is that we are mere reflections. We brought something to the world too. In fact, we brought a lot."

"Of course, you did," the priest agreed. "Any good child brings more to the world than he gets from the parents. Although you may be unaware of the greatest thing you brought."

"What is it?" Nil asked, surprised with the change of the tone.

"Mass entertainment, your games," the priest said. "Nobody before managed to do something like that. We had religious celebrations but that's different, too mandatory. Greeks had their Olympic games but they were rare. And their theatre… it's a rather elitist thing. You are the first to consume the masses with such a mind-numbing experience. Your plebs just sleep, eat, work, and whatever time is left is consumed by the entertainment, effectively taking them out of the political equation. That's a wonderful invention. The only thing that beats it would be to bring the entertainment directly into each of their huts, making working people disappear from the streets altogether. Sleep, work, eat, entertain, sleep, work, eat, entertain, a perfect cycle for human animals. You Romans are unsurpassed in this achievement. Of course, other children had their contributions as well."

"Other?"

"Yes," the priest said. "Let's see. Jews invented a jealous God. Wonderful, absolutely wonderful invention. For forty centuries we could not make everybody believe in the one and only God, and they did it. A janitor, a tailor, a brick maker, even a toilet cleaner, they all believe in one God. It's a pity this will not work in an empire – too many people, too different."

"So, this one is lost," Nil said. "Right?"

"Absolutely not," the priest said and solemnly shook the head. "Their offshoot, these Christians, they brought another wonderful invention – the loving God, son of the jealous God, still the same God. I don't know who can beat that. Nobody. Think about it: God, who sacrificed his own son to ensure forgiveness and eternal life for every human. God, who loves every man, woman, and child in the world. God, who grieves over every quarry worker, every widow, every hungry infant. In fact, you may be right, Rome will face the fire. Not just Rome, the whole world around us. Those Christians, they are going to take the world like fire. All this thanks to the resurrected loving God."

"I see," Nil said. "Resurrection is their new idea, right?"

"Not exactly," the priest said. "Osiris resurrected to rule the underworld and to care for the afterlife of our people. Re is traveling underworld every night and raising up every morning alive and well. Resurrection is an old idea. An omnipotent God who is human and loving – that's really new and all powerful. I only don't understand why you don't like them."

"Whom?" Nil asked. "Christians?"

"Yes," the priest said. "They are perfect for you. A loving caring God who is conveniently where the God should be, in the heavens. And who represents him on Earth?"

Nil did not say a thing expecting the priest to continue his monologue.

"The emperor!" the priest said. "It's even better than a divine emperor, because if you are divine, you should show some miracles. In fact, that's part of the reason behind building those pyramids. And if you are just a human appointed by the God? Nothing. You don't possess any powers and, still, you are entitled to a complete and unconditional obedience. Your God is omnipotent, he would not allow him to be a ruler if he did not want that. And if the ruler is bad, well, apparently he is sent to you in punishment, it still does not change a thing. It's a perfect religion for an empire."

"But how do you call them your children? Both Jews and Christians despise Egypt," Nil said.

"Just like many other children do to their parents when they grow up. So what?" the priest said. "For reference, the founder of Christians was brought here," he pointed his finger down, "to this city as a newly born infant. He was grown here until the king in Judea died and they could return." He smiled at his thoughts and then laughed light-heartedly. "Jews are slaughtering bulls in their temple to show how different they are from us. And those Mithraist Persians, they built their whole mythology around the sacrifice of a bull. How cute – the bravery of the young. Actually, they are very good kids too."

"I thought you worship bulls," Nil said. "I know, I know, that's a bullshit, still I don't understand."

"No, we don't worship bulls," the priest said. "Commoners do. Commoners worship bulls, gods, sky, sea. Everything that may bring harm, they fear, and everything they fear they worship. That's how our kings became 'gods'. That's why the jealous God does not work in an empire. If you have a small country, all your people are of the same origin, and if somebody wants to worship something strange, what do you do? You can despise them, cut them from the trade and other people, or even kill them. In a small country, you can solve this problem. And what if you rule an Empire? Too bad, too many of your subjects believe in odd things and are ready to die for them. You despise them and they revolt. You kill them, and you have nobody to rule."

"I don't think it's a problem," Nil said. "You fared very well for a while, and so do we. Anyway, who cares about commoners?"

"That's what we do here. In this land we have consecrates, who know the truth, and commoners, who are free to worship whatever they fancy. And through the state and commoners' cults, the consecrates rule them and keep their behavior socially acceptable. Those Zoroaster Persians do the same. Jews don't have an empire on their hands, neither do Greeks. But, you see, you have to care for commoners. Because sometimes, really smart and strong people are born between them. And if you treat them as commoners, they become leaders. And then your commoners revolt, and that's nasty. You need to get these strong and smart commoners into consecrates. Here, in this land, a commoner who is smart and moral and insistent may become a consecrate. Unfortunately, most of them are neither smart, nor moral. And it's not easy if the truth is a secret, and they are raised to believe in false gods."

"Did I become a consecrate?" Nil asked. "I don't remember that, but you tell me all this stuff."

"Not yet," the priest said. "It's like in those Christians stories, death cleans, forgives, rebirth gives another chance. Crucifixion-resurrection, death-rebirth, sunset-sunrise. That's why I wanted you to be at the sunset ceremony. You were cleaned, and now it only depends on you who will see the rising sun tomorrow with your eyes."

"But why me?" Nil asked. "I came here on an odd mission, asked some pretty stupid questions, and now, all of the sudden, you are initiating me into your secrets?"

"Because you are very promising," the priest said. "I tested you, Nil. I watched your reactions, and listened to your words, even if it did not look so. You are smart. And you are not just doing your job, you serve. And, I believe, you don't serve the emperor, you serve the Empire. And that's the next best thing after serving God, the real God. In fact, sometimes, it's the same."

"How so?"

"Empires are not about emperors, they are about people. You sow the seeds, you wait until they grow. Then savages come from Deshret and rob you. How do you protect yourself? By pulling together with other people. If savages are numerous, you have to be numerous too. If the year is bad and you don't have crops, what do you do? You die. Unless, of course, somebody saved some grain from the last year, and now gives it to you. Who pulls the army to defend from savages? Who saves the grain to survive a bad year? The state, the Empire. Empire serves people. Serve the Empire, and you serve the people."

"A lot of people don't live under Rome, and they're doing seemingly well," Nil argued.

"Not every land is Kemet, not every land is Rome. There are places where you can have crops year after the year, no hassle, no worries. You just stick a dry cane into the ground and it sprouts with fruits. And your enemies are the neighbor family, as small and weak as yours. Then you don't need an empire, and you live in your small families, like they do in Canaan, or in small cities, like Greeks. Only its not for long. Sooner or later strong and numerous savages still come to your land, and if you are not ready, greedy barbarians rule you one after another, robbing you of your fruits, and usually much more than that. That's what was going on in the northern land between Tigris and Euphrates for millennia. If you are lucky enough, an empire comes and defends you against the barbarians. If you are smart like the Greeks, you embrace it and benefit from it."

"The land between Tigris and Euphrates is ruled by Parthia, right?"

"And before that, Persia. And before that, Babylon. And before that, Assyria. But they are not empires. There are only two principles of the state in the world – the state for the people, and the people for the state. When a single ruler exists, the first is called monarchy, the second is tyranny. The state for the people creates empires. They are long-lasting because the state and the people support each other, becoming stronger and stronger. The second type is not an empire, it's just savages who conquered enough land to rob. Their states die as soon as they rob the people of everything the people have. Then there is nothing to rob anymore and the whole point of their state disappears."

"Still, how is it the same as serving God?"

"Look at the false gods of this land," the priest said. "Most of them are supposed to be the children of one main god, right? They are actually individual sides of God, like his might, his strength, his love, but only consecrates understand that. For commoners they are just children of God. That's the only reason they are worshipped at all. And people are the children of the real God. So serving the people, you serve the children of God. The only difference from the crowd is that you serve the real children of the real God."

"That's all fascinating," Nil said. "But I still don't see how it relates to me."

"Two reasons," the priest said. "First, you asked for that. You understood something about this particular situation you have on your hands now. You need to decide what to do. Don't you feel it touches some important springs and gears making the Roman Empire work? If so, you need to understand these springs and gears, right?"

"Possibly," Nil said. "What's the second reason?"

"Purpose-questions-answers, remember?" the priest asked. He was not dispassionate anymore. He looked Nil straight in the eyes with a tenacious, alert expression. "You looked for a mission. I may have one for you."

Nil did not say anything, not knowing what to say.

"Look, you've got quite enough for one day," the priest said. "I suspect your head is spinning right now and you need to understand a thing or two. Go home now. Sleep. Sleep well. In the morning, don't go interrogating the local priests, it's a waste of time. Explain to Simaat that I told you to do so. Go to a tavern, have some wine. We make great wine here in Kemet. Think. You may talk to Simaat, if you want. He is a high ranking priest; he knows a lot. Think for a day. Have a good night sleep again. Go to the tavern and think again. And if you still feel like coming back, come here one hour before sunset. And we will talk again."

They went down the stairway. A junior priest was waiting for them.

"Accompany our guest to the inn," the Great Seer ordered.

"I don't need a guard," Nil said.

"Of course," the Great Seer smiled. "But you need a torch and somebody who knows the city." He waived his hand to Nil and went out.

It was almost the middle of the night when Nil got to the inn. The Great Seer was right, Nil's head was spinning and it was hard to make much sense from the mess that filled his mind now. Simaat was soundly asleep, so without further conversations, Nil took off his armor and laid down on the floor with his cloak as a bed sheet. Egyptians did not fancy couches or any other risen places except the benches around the wall, at least not in this inn. And then he went to sleep, leaving the gladius nearby, just in case.

EMPEROR THE WHO?
Chapter XX, where senator Albinus is not happy with the emperor and Nil learns to master the roads

"Mithra!" Seven feet tall *Running on the Sun* Gaius Albinus Leon, a patrician and senator, roared through his clenched teeth and hit the writing table with his heavy fist. The table was heavy and made of old oak so it survived. Gaius looked around to see that nobody was close by. The cult of Mithra was secret, its members were not supposed to shout his name in the presence of anybody uninitiated. Only his friend, Levton, was sitting on a couch nearby. That was ok, Levton was *Persian*. Not a Persian from Persia, that was his rank in the brotherhood.

"Interesting news?" Levton asked with a laugh. He was a Greek, less than thirty years old with dark smart eyes and a carefully trimmed beard and moustache, framing his regular, lean face.

"See this letter from Lucceius?" Gaius said, showing the scroll of papyrus that he was holding in his hand. "You know where he is now, right?"

"Lucceius Albinus? He is the procurator of Judea," Levton said. "Thanks to your benevolence and the brotherhood's help. Why?"

"Read it," Gaius said and passed the letter.

Levton read it through. "Interesting, Christians burning Rome with the help of Jews and Egyptians."

"Do you believe it?" Gaius asked.

"What? About Christians or about burning Rome?"

"Yes, I also don't think this pathetic rabble has anything to do with an arson," Gaius said.

"But you also suspect that Rome will burn, just the way Lucceius reports?" Levton asked.

"How long will this pluck of a dog rule the empire? He is not even an Augustus. He was adopted by Claudius, who was persuaded in bed by his mother just to be killed by her poison."

"Well, she paid for that. He killed her right after his coming of age," Levton said. "Do you think it's him?"

"Who else?" Gaius said. "Did you hear, he wants a new large palace, right on Palatine, going up to Esquiline Hill. And where will he get the space for a palace?"

"So he decided to clean some space with a fire," Levton said. "And who cares if some people burn?"

"We care, *Persian*," Gaius said with low voice.

"I know, *Running on the Sun*," Levton agreed. "But he does not."

"His sins exceeded all measures," Gaius said.

"He has to go," Levton agreed. "Can we do anything about the fire?"

"Probably, nothing," Gaius said. "If his dog, Tigellinus, arranges it, we have no control over the execution of such a plan."

"But we can use the fire," Levton said. "If the people learn that he did it…"

"He will be gone," Gaius finished. "For good."

"Give him enough rope," Levton smiled.

"To hang himself," Gaius nodded.

"We need to bring it to the council of the brotherhood," Levton said.

"Truly so," Gaius agreed.

"What if Rome does not burn?" Levton asked.

"How?"

"What if Lucceius is wrong?" Gaius said. "Or what if Tigellinus does not succeed? We need a backup plan to present to the council."

"You are right," Gaius agreed. "Tigellinus is only good to make silly accusations and kill innocent people. And, of course, organize orgies on the Agrippa's lake."

"In a sense, that's what he is going to do here too," Levton said. "That is, kill innocent people."

"True," Gaius agreed. "But he still may fail, and then we need another plan."

"Tell me if I am out of line, *Running on the Sun…*" Levton said.

Gaius just looked at him, waiting for the question.

"Could a few *Warriors* lend a hand to Tigellinus' people, to make sure Rome burns?" Levton said. "And they can do that to Tigellinus' palace, returning the fire to the incendiary."

"And making it even more suspicious to the public," Gaius agreed.

Levton nodded with a chuckle.

"First, we need a council to decide that the brotherhood will need to get rid of him," Gaius said.

"That should be easy," Levton said. "This scumbag is the most hated person in the empire, unless you count Tigellinus as a person."

"So be it, *Persian*," Gaius said.

"So be it, *Running on the Sun*."

* * *

Two days passed. There was again the dark passage, the Sun shining on the benben stone, the priest at the altar, and an unhurried walk on the Temple wall.

"So, you are back," the priest said.

"You were right," Nil said. "All my life I served the empire, not the emperor. That's my life, and that's my honor."

"Have you decided anything?"

"Frankly, I am lost," Nil said. "I don't want a part in organizing the fire, and I cannot prevent the fire. I don't know what to do."

"You are asking the wrong questions," the priest said. "Remember, start from the purpose. You said you serve the empire. Should you prevent the fire?"

"Shouldn't I?" Nil asked.

"Who'd like to see Rome burned?" the priest asked.

"Tigellinus," Nil said. "Maybe the emperor too."

"Who else?"

"Too many," Nil said after a moments thought. "Almost everybody would try, if they were not afraid."

"And if the empire shows a weakness?"

"They will attack, like a pack of jackals would attack a sick lion."

"So, who made the lion sick?" the priest asked patiently.

"Tigellinus, the prefect?" Nil asked.

The priest only shook his head.

"The emperor?" Nil said, surprised himself with what he had said.

"Yes," the priest answered. "He is not fit to rule the empire. He is weak, and jealous, and foolish. So what should people who try to save the empire, do?"

"Depose the emperor?" Nil asked. "Assuming these people can do that."

"Can *you* do that?"

"No," Nil admitted. "I am nobody."

"Sometimes, and very often, nobody is much more than somebody," the priest smiled. "But you're right – to serve the empire you need the power. The more challenge you face, the more power you need. And what is the ultimate power in an empire? Aside from God, of course?"

"The emperor?" Nil asked.

The priest slowly shook his head. He turned to the moonlit landscape outside, standing erect and recalling something.

"There were the times when we used to appoint the kings in this land," he said at last.

"Isn't it in God's hands?" Nil asked.

"Yes. But He needs the tools to do that... human tools," the priest said. "Why not you? Raise the new emperor, get rid of the old one, and your empire will see the next day."

"The next day?" Nil chuckled joylessly. "Not so much."

"What do you want?" the priest said and shrugged his shoulders. "Every night Re fights the great snake Apophis, so that he could rise again in the morning, and so that we will see another day. He does not have to do so. He could settle down in the underworld and be quite comfortable there. But he fights so that we can see another day. Just one more day. Because the next day, he will have to fight again. Did you hope for more for yourself? That's all you can do. To give your people one more day. And this new day will bring new battles."

"With the new emperor it may be more than one day," Nil said.

"Sure," the priest agreed. "It could be a few decades of prosperity. Just don't count on that and be ready."

"But I don't know how to do this task," Nil said.

"Does it mean that you take it?" the priest asked.

"It sounds like an honorable thing even to try," Nil admitted. "What's your interest in giving Rome 'another day'?"

"It's your interest," the priest said. "Rome is our offspring, but we are not so much interested in Rome as we are interested in you."

"Me?!" Nil said dumb struck by such a statement. "Forgive me, but who am I to be of any interest to you?"

"Sure, I forgive you," the priest said with a relaxed smile.

"And can you explain?" Nil asked after he recognized the joke.

"You see, empires live differently than people," the priest said. "At some point they overgrow their bodily appearance and become spirits, powerful spirits brought around by people and influencing other lands. That's what happened to Kemet. We overgrew our land, and borders, and armies. People are carrying our spirit to the farthest ends of the world. Our offspring flourishes, growing into new lands, new people, new empires. Jews have our way of life, our knowledge of living in an empire. They left Egypt, but they brought Kemet in their hearts and souls, and they will bring Kemet with them wherever they go. You Romans took the other part of our spirit, a very important part, the spirit of the Empire – maybe one of the most precious sides. Parthians lately got the idea of the benevolent rule and power. Not that they mastered it, but at least they have it. This is also very important. Christians and Jews will spread the idea of one true God around, and I wish them every success in that. But one side of Kemet is missing, one very, very important part."

He came close to the parapet on the outer side of the wall.

"The Temple," the priest said and tapped the stones. Sand spilled from the parapet under his hand. "These stones served us well for millennia. It helped to control pagans and keep them not far away from morality and good. Now that Kemet is a spirit, it cannot use a stone temple anymore. Christians and Jews will bring the idea of the true God to people, but that's about making pagans believe in one God. That would be a great achievement, but the world will still need the consecrates, the Temple, to keep them on track. Not to rule others, we never did that, not to point others how to believe, but to prevent the unfortunate turns of life such as what happened now, to keep monsters off the power, to give people another day. In the spiritual Kemet to come, people will need a spiritual temple, made of people, not stones."

"So you want me to be a stone in your temple?" Nil asked.

"No, you already are," the priest smiled. "And anyway, one stone is too little; you need many of them. That's what Jews and Christians will do – they will provide the bricks for the spiritual Temple. They are very good at it. If I remember their sacred texts right, that's what they did here. But the stones don't come into the Temple by themselves, and stones certainly don't come into the Temple by themselves *right*. You need to be sure that you are building the Temple, not a ramshackle hut ready to crush down because of the slanted shaky walls and lack of a plan. It needs an architect, an engineer, a mason. And more than one, actually."

"I see that you are not of very high opinion about Jews and Christians," Nil said. "Brick makers?"

"Don't be arrogant," the priest said. "That's a lot. When your bricks are people, that is the most important part. Only by respecting them, can you succeed in your own mission."

"Fine. But what do I get?" Nil asked.

"Our knowledge, our wisdom, our power," the priest said. "To give your people another day."

"Why me?" Nil asked. "I admit, it's tempting, but why me?"

"Because, it's your mission," the priest said. "That's why you came to this world – to give your people another day. Remember, I told you that I would talk to stars about you? I did."

"Am I the only one?" Nil asked.

"It depends," the priest said. "Your mission is just one side of the spiritual Kemet. Within it, you are one with Romans, with Jews, with Parhians, with Christians, even with Greeks. Are you the only one in your special side? No. You will need followers, you will need allies. Are we talking to anybody else? Yes, sometimes. We are very selective, and the person should ask himself, even before he is told what to ask. What if somebody else comes here and asks? I may talk to him. And if he is the right man, I may send him to you, or I may give him another mission. It all depends on the stars and God's will. Anyway, as I said – you asked for a purpose, a mission of your life, I have one for you. Do you take it?"

"I have to go back soon," Nil said. "I cannot stay to learn."

"Of course, you cannot. You have a mission to do, remember? Don't worry, we can send our people with advice for you," the priest said. "Anyway, we are not going down so soon, you and your followers will still have a century or two to learn from us."

"So, what now," Nil asked. "An initiation, mystic places, clandestine rites?"

"No, not for you," the priest laughed softly. "You have an immediate mission, remember? To give Rome another day."

"Still, no initiation, no rite? Does not sound Egyptian…"

"I can send a few Temple girls to dance in front of you and Simaat, if you need some rite that it will make you feel better," the priest shrugged his shoulders. "I think, your problem with rites is exactly the same as with false gods: you just don't know that they are highly optional to say the least."

"Why?"

"Both false gods and rites are supposed to keep commoners in control and out of sacred knowledge until they are ready for it," the priest said. "These are the tools. You need to learn how to use these tools, but you don't have to try them out yourself. A dentist knows how to extract a sick tooth, but he does not take out his own healthy teeth just because he is a dentist. After all, you came to this world with this mission, your soul was sent by God to do exactly that. What extra initiation do you need after that?"

Nil scratched his head and did not say anything.

"Good," the priest said. "Now about your direct mission. I cannot tell you what to do, it's your job. But I can help you find the right questions and the right answers, as well as give advice, which you are free to follow or abandon. I am not your superior – I don't give orders. You are only responsible to God for what you do. We hope to raise a child of Kemet, not another slave. A child who will be well and alive when this stone temple is long gone. Is that understood?"

"I would not take your orders even if you try to give them," Nil said. "But I'll listen to your advice and give a good thinking to it."

"Perfect," the priest said with an almost happy smile. "That's what I would expect from a son with a promise of greatness. So, what do you think is the main sickness that endangers Rome?"

"The emperor," Nil said, somewhat amused at how easily he said that.

"Truly so," the priest agreed. "He is trying to convert your Empire into a mere robber state like Babylon. And robber states don't last long. Now what do you have to do?"

"Get rid of him."

"How do you know that the next one will be better?"

"I hope–"

"A very stupid answer, Nil," the priest interrupted him. "You might as well hope that he will die tomorrow all by himself. Hopes are for no-doers. How do you make it happen?"

"Are you saying that I should find the new emperor?"

"You need to make sure the new emperor is better than this one," the priest said. "That's for sure."

"How do I do that?"

"You cannot do that."

"But you said that I should, right?"

"You cannot do that by yourself," the priest explained. "That's the way in politics, you don't do something yourself, you make others do what you want for yourself."

"Whom?"

"The senate, the people of Rome," the priest shrugged his shoulders. "And you cannot make them do that by yourself either."

"So do how I do that?"

"By getting allies," the priest said. "By aligning with the people who want the same or almost the same. Then you influence them to correct their actions just a little, to match what you want. You cannot change it a lot, well, in some cases you can, but it's usually not worth the effort. Just a little is all you need if they already want the things to be almost the same as you do."

"And then helping them, right?"

"Not necessary," the priest said. "If you closely associate yourself with somebody, you may become one of them, and then your options will be limited. Keeping a distance from all your allies gives you a freedom to get more allies, including allies for other tasks. And remember – never do a job that somebody else can do. Spend your time finding others who can do the job that you need. That's what is important."

"That's smart," Nil agreed. "But how do I find them."

"By trying. You'll learn with time," the priest said. "By the way, spend a few days with Simaat discussing your problems. He is very good at this stuff. He may help you with ideas where to find the allies and how to influence them. There is a proverb: ask the people to do what they love to do, and you will not have to work for the rest of your life."

Nil smiled. "I'd love to."

"I thought you would," the priest said. "Now, before 'how to do', let us see if we are crystal clear about 'what to do'?"

"We need to get rid of the emperor," Nil said. "And we need to find and crown the new emperor, someone who will be good for the Empire."

"And now, what about the fire?"

"I don't think I can prevent it," Nil said.

"But can you use it?"

The conversation went long, almost until the morning. Nil spent a few more days talking to the Great Seer at nights and Simaat during the day. On the seventh day, he and Simaat left to Alexandria.

* * *

Again there was a silence under the huge moon covering the endless marshes surrounding the river. Nil woke up from the scream of a bird caught in its nest by a crocodile. The boat was almost the same size as the one that brought Nil to On. It was one of the last ships this season bringing the grain down the river to be shipped to the capital, to the Great Rome, to feed its shouting crowds.

Nil shook his head. What the hell, he thought, did I agree to do just a few days ago? Depose the emperor? Me? Have I gone crazy? He clasped his head in his hands. That's the emperor!

What happened to me? How did I agree to such a thing? They will smash me like a fly and will not even notice...

He looked around. The great silence surrounded the ship. This world was magnificent, mighty, and it knew it. It felt like it was asking: emperor the who? Really, Nil thought, who? That pimply hoarse bastard? He chuckled and looked around again. This world was really mighty; even the air breathed with the power and purpose. It felt even stronger than several days ago on the way up. But now it was not threatening anymore. Nil felt all this might and power behind him, supporting him, filling him. Emperor, the who?

He recalled one of the last conversations with the Great Seer.

"Is not it a grand task for one man?" Nil asked.

"You are not one," the priest said. "You will find allies. And remember, no matter how great a task looks, a road will be conquered by walking."

"A somewhat cryptic message, isn't it?"

"It means that you have to walk to walk the road over, and there is no other way," the priest said.

"How?" Nil asked.

"One step at a time."

ZE GRIEF OF YOUR PEOPLE
Chapter XXI, where the wish of so many comes true

The morning of the third day of September Ides was not remarkable in any way. Just another day. People were eating, sleeping, making love, and making enemies, talking, shouting, trading, and wasting their lives in innumerable other ways as usual. The emperor was not in the city. He went to his suburban residence in Actium to relax and have some time away from his busy schedule. Some would say from the busy schedule of binges, orgies, and executing more innocent people, but anyway, he was not in the city following Tigellinus' advice. After all, they knew the day, so who would suspect the emperor if he was not even around to give such an order? Not that he gave such an order, of course.

The day passed uneventfully and the sun began to set. When the last ray went off, many interesting and visibly unrelated events started to unroll under the dim reddish light of the evening dusk.

* * *

Followers of Seamus gathered on the corner near the circus. Each of them brought a piece of wood, and Seamus brought a jug of oil. They put the wood together, ignoring passers-by. Passers-by ignored them as well. Who cared if a small group of slaves made a little heap of wood in the middle of the road, unless they were in your way? Maybe they are ordered to fix the road? Everybody had their own business to attend.

Seamus started a speech with curses towards the city and promises of the eternal life for everybody who joined him. Now some of the people on the street started to look his way occasionally, and a couple of poorly dressed gapers joined the group, staring at the leader and listening to him. Most of the people, however, hurriedly passed by ignoring wailing and shouting now produced by the group. The Roman public was busy, and who cares if a small group of bozos tries to preach on the street? You definitely don't want to be involved.

Meanwhile Seamus oiled the wood, spilling enough on the pavement around as well. Then he slipped on the oil and it took some time to get the wood back into the heap. By this time his tunic absorbed most of the oil from the wood, so they had to repeat oiling again. Luckily, one of the followers was enthusiastic enough to bring another jar of oil with him. Carefully balancing to avoid slipping again, Seamus took a torch and raised it high in his hand.

"Now comes the time, brothers," he howled, "when this dirty city is gone for good in the wrath of God! Watch it go, brothers!"

He put the torch down and his tunic burst into flames. Nobody moved. The followers waited for the leader to fire up the wood, and the staring passers-by decided that this was part of the performance. In fact, now more people passing by stopped and started to stare. You don't see a live person bursting into flames every day. That was exciting and interesting, almost as exciting and interesting as the games. The crowd started to whistle and applaud. Seamus, meanwhile, was rolling on the ground and shouting, so in a few seconds followers realized that something had not gone by the plan. As it was not completely clear to them what the plan was, they started to shout too, adding confusion to the whole mess.

Seamus would probably have suffered greatly, but three vigils, who passed by, broke to him through the crowd and put the fire out to the great disappointment of the public gathered around. Somebody even threw an apple core at the vigils. Anyway, the vigils were not on the job now, they were just going to a tavern. They did not bother to investigate what happened or detain the strange man who almost burnt himself right on the street. They had more important things to do. Only the youngest one delayed long enough to spit on Seamus, and run after his friends already entering the tavern.

The crowd started to disperse, discussing the event, some excitedly, some with disappointment. A detachment of Praetorian Guards passed by, moving to the area behind the river where many of the Christians lived. They did not pay any attention to the group of poorly dressed perplexed people surrounding a man with heavy burns over his body. They were busy fulfilling the order of arresting Christian incendiaries who lived on another bank of Tiber.

* * *

Bokha's people gathered in front of the Dragon's store and warehouse. Along the street they saw the corner with Seamus and his people. When they saw the flames and heard the shouting of the crowd, they rushed into the store, as Bokha said, to make the final payments to the old foe and competitor. Surprisingly, there was nobody in the store, so the task became very easy to achieve.

It actually would not be so surprising if they'd known that Dragon's people had, at the same time, assembled on another side from the same corner in front of the Bokha's store. Understandably, there was nobody in this store either.

* * *

Hludwick was not with Seamus that night. He was sent on a mission by his master, Doctor Noot, and the mission was pretty much the same as the one that Seamus was trying to achieve. Not that he did not try to be with Seamus, but when he asked the master for the night off, he was deeply disappointed. He even started to worry about the salvation of his soul. That's, of course, until he knew what the master wanted him to do that night. Hludwick even double-checked with Seamus – no, there should be absolutely no problem with salvation, the prophet confirmed.

Hludwick and two other slaves quietly came to the house of ben Ata Khin. One man threw a jar of oil into the dark window of the first floor. Another accompanied it with a burning torch. They quickly turned around the corner and repeated the procedure. Then they disappeared in the darkness.

Doctor Noot and Doctor ben Ata, meanwhile, were in the residence of the Roman Dental and Plumbing Association. The ceremony of initiation of new members had just finished and the leaders of the two factions were engaged in peaceful and friendly conversation, both with goblets of wine in their hands.

"It was a great year for all of us. For our prosperity, dear colleague," Doctor Noot said, raising the goblet.

"It surely was. For our prosperity, Doctor," ben Ata said with a well-disposed smile and raised his wine.

Benjamin was not at home in Tigellinus' palace this night. Together with ben Ata's servant, he was approaching Doctor Noot's house. They showed more sophistication than Hludwick

– ben Ata paid for a few pouches of the Greek fire, a highly flammable substance sometimes used in military operations. When the fiery pouches disappeared in the dark window, both turned and walked away, ignoring the yellow glares starting to grow inside the house.

* * *

Maalish looked around a small room that he had rented just few days ago. The floor and walls were well oiled and ready. He stepped closer to the door and smiled slightly with the ends of his lips. The prince would be satisfied.

He took a piece of oiled fabric, lit it up from the lamp, and dropped it on the floor. Then he looked around, slowly left the room, closed the door behind him, and walked away by the dark street.

He knew that a dozen of his people did the same in several places around the city, take or add half an hour. He knew that by now, they had all left the doomed houses and walked to the secret meeting place in the far corner of the city.

* * *

Three *sicaries*, an extreme faction of zealots, were going along one of the back streets. They were choosing black windows, whose inhabitants were either not home or already sleeping. The torches they used were a variation of oil lamps, so after being thrown into windows they were spilling everything around with blazing drops of oil. Eleazar suggested the idea when sending them to Rome.

"And remember," he said with a smile, "you are sent there to *not* do that."

Not too many, anyway. They managed to do it only to three houses before people started to run out to the street, crying and looking for incendiaries. Then all three dived out into a narrow lane, ran away, and then repeated it on another street. Any other day, they would be quickly caught by vigils and guards, but this day was special, and vigils were already busy.

* * *

A group of zealots led by Shaul and financed by Temah were doing about the same behind the river, in the area densely populated by Christians. They were choosing wooden houses, dry as firewood after the hot summer, putting some flammable stuff, usually some straw, on the back of the house, where it was not visible from the street. Then they fired it up and moved to the next target, leaving it to the divine will to make the fire grow or die.

* * *

People of Galen gathered near the spot that Lucius Vistinus – the prefect of Egypt – picked for himself. The actual spot was on the top of the hill with rich residences, wide yards, guard dogs, and slaves who could put a small fire out all by themselves. So instead they came to the foot of the hill, where poor two- and three-story multifamily dwellings were crumbled upon each other. Galen figured that if these houses caught fire, the flame would easily climb from one house to another to the top of the hill, cleaning the whole place.

Dressed as vigils, they went along the street, looking for the dark windows. They spotted one and went to the door. Galen knocked loudly at the door to the apartment, and curious faces appeared in the windows across the street.

"By the order of Caesar!" Galen demanded loudly and knocked again.

The faces quickly disappeared. Nobody wanted to be involved. Galen broke the door and they entered. The apartment was empty, apparently the tenants were not here at the moment. Galen's men spilled oil across the room and added two pouches of burning Greek fire as a starter. Then they all left the building and moved along the street.

They passed a dozen houses before repeating the procedure. Now the apartment was not empty. An old man – probably some low level scribe or maybe even a slave of the missing tenant – was soundly asleep when they came in.

"You are arrested by the order of Caesar for attempt of arson," Galen loudly declared, so that all the neighbors heard it. The old man fell on his knees, shaking and begging for mercy. Two of Galen's men took him out to the street, while the rest repeated manipulations with the oil and Greek fire without witnesses, and left after closing the door behind. Now, Galen thought with a smile, the blame would be put on the tenant. Everybody will think that "vigils" just missed a spot and left some fire alive. They passed about a dozen more houses when Galen grabbed the old man by the collar.

"Look, father," he said. "I don't believe you really did anything wrong, so here is your chance – run. And don't return home or you will be arrested."

He let the old man go, who obediently stumped into the narrow lane without asking any questions. Galen chuckled with satisfaction for his own smartness. No, he did not invent this way to spread the fire. It was actually Nil who described it after he returned from Heliopolis. All Galen had to do was ask, with a naïve look in his eyes, how was it possible to set a great city on fire? No, really, how? It's beyond what mortals can do. Galen recalled with a smile how the stupid Roman shrugged his shoulders and provided step-by-step instructions without a clue that they would really be used.

The first house already caught fire, so they passed two more blocks before picking the next target.

* * *

Nobody saw how or when the heavy draperies in the private dining room of the emperor caught fire. In fact, nobody noticed it until the whole room was in flames and the fire spread outside. In less than an hour, most of the palace was burning and the fire was spreading further.

* * *

When Tigellinus arrived in the city, more than a third of it was already on fire. According to witnesses, the fire started in a couple of stores located near the circus. Then it spread all over the city.

There was a moment when it looked like vigils and citizens managed to contain the fire. The great damage was already done, but there was a hope to stop it now. Then, to the surprise of Tigellinus, the fire started again in his own palace and spread around the city with all its elemental fury.

* * *

The emperor interrupted his stay in Actium and got back. It was the night when he reached the city walls. The imperial procession could not get into the city because it was on fire so they stopped before the gates. The emperor and his escort went to the nearby heights. The city was visible from this place to the farthest ends. It was brightly lit by fires covering about two thirds of it with the hot orange glow. The smoke going up and lit by the fire formed queer shapes in the air. Small figures of men and women were running on the streets, some trying to extinguish the flame, some just trying to run from it.

The emperor stood at the edge of the hill. Tigellinus and Poppaea were by his sides and a little behind. Dismayed by the view, Poppaea pressed her hands against her chest, motionlessly watching with wide open eyes. In contrast, Tigellinus stood completely unmoved and relaxed, viewing the city with a vacant look and expecting the emperor to make the decisions.

"Such a tragedy," the emperor said solemnly at last. "Truly a great tragedy that will be foretold by future generations with awe and reverence. I probably should honor my people with a song now. The one which I devoted to the Fall of Troy."

Poppaea looked at him, surprised, then slowly shook her head behind his back without saying a word.

"Should we try to take care of survivors?" Tigellinus asked. "Something like ordering food delivery and distribution, and maybe opening some parks to live in until the city can be rebuilt?"

"Yes," the emperor said. "Do that. Open all my private parks for people."

A soldier in the red cloak of a Praetorian Guard, with soot on his face, approached the group.

"I was sent with a message to the prefect," he said.

"Talk," the emperor commanded.

"The witnesses say there are people on the streets throwing torches into windows and shouting that they do it by the order of Caesar," the soldier said. "A few survivors also claim that these people are Praetorians in civil cloths."

The emperor turned to Tigellinus. "Did you give such an order?!"

"No, Caesar," the prefect said. "How could I? I remember your orders!"

"Then who are these people?"

"How do I know?" Tigellinus said and turned to the messenger with a gloomy look.

"I did not see these people myself," the soldier said, trying to appear not scared. "I've seen people claiming that, and my commander thought that you'd prefer to know."

The emperor dismissed the messenger, who disappeared at once with visible relief, and turned to Tigellinus.

"I hope this has nothing to do with that money Galba is going to raise now?" he said with a low voice.

"I almost told this money good bye already, when the message of fire came in," Tigellinus said almost sincerely.

Another man approached the emperor. He was dressed as a northeastern barbarian, probably Skyph or Sarmat, with the gold rings and bracelets on his hands and a silver neckpiece with gems.

"Ze sing and ruler of Hyperborea sends his sincere condolences to Caesar, ze great ruler of Rome," he said with a deep bow, burring the words with a weird accent.

"Who, the hell, is that?" the emperor asked with a puzzled expression on his face and pointing to the man with his little finger.

"I am ze ambassador of his Majesty Sing of Hyperborea, extraordinary and plenipotentiary," the man said with another low bow. "His Majesty asked me to say that he never quarrels with Rome and feels ze grief of your people."

"I thought Hyperborea only exists in the tales of drunken sailors," the emperor looked at Tigellinus. The prefect said nothing, puzzled as much as everybody else.

"Vee are not ze tales of drunken zailors," the man said with a wide smile and another bow. "Vee are ze land on ze north, far far on ze north. And vee are really sympathize with your tragedy."

"How?" the emperor asked. "How did you know about that?" He pointed with his hand to the burning city.

"Zis is hard to miss," the man said with another bow. "You see? Zis is very well visible from far around."

"How long have you traveled to Rome?" the emperor asked.

"More zan three months," the man said proudly. "Zis was a very very long and hard way, and I had to hurry to come in time."

The emperor sat on the folding chair, brought by somebody from the retinue, clasped his hands around his head, and quietly

171

moaned. Tigellinus made a sign, and a soldier from the escort took the ambassador, extraordinary and plenipotentiary, by the collar and pushed him behind the retinue, standing in a semicircle just few steps behind the emperor.

Tigellinus, relaxed and self-assured, glanced to the city submerged in the fire.

"Don't worry, Caesar," he said. "Rome is great and strong. It will be born again from these ashes, as great and as mighty as ever. My men are already arresting the ones who performed the arson. And about the one who devised such a plan and put it in motion... we will find him and he will pay for this crime. I had a man who never failed me before. He will find this criminal and bring him to justice. My man's name is Nil Septimus, and he never, really never, failed me before."

The Emperor Nero was sitting on the folding chair at the edge of the hill, clasping his head in his hands, quietly moaning, and looking at the great fire of Rome.